'Why are you being so nice?' she whispered.

Because you're the love of my life and I hate to see you hurting. I want to make you feel better. Not that he was going to tell her that. It wasn't the right time. 'Because I care, Tally. Whatever's happened between us, I still care.' He still loved her. And he always would.

Somehow—Kit couldn't even remember moving—he was sitting down, on his own chair this time, and Natalie was sitting on his lap. Her arms were round his neck, her fingers sliding into his hair. And he was kissing her eyelids, tiny butterfly kisses brushing down to the corners of her eyes, her temples. The lightest, lightest touch. A moth's wing against a candle flame.

And he was burning.

'Kit...'

But her voice wasn't saying *stop*. It was saying *go on*.

Kate Hardy lives in Norwich, in the east of England, with her husband, two young children, one bouncy spaniel, and too many books to count! When she's not busy writing romance or researching local history, she helps out at her children's schools; she's a school governor and chair of the PTA. She also loves cooking—see if you can spot the recipes sneaked into her books! (They're also on her website, along with extracts and stories behind the books.) Writing for Mills & Boon® has been a dream come true for Kate—something she's wanted to do ever since she was twelve. She's been writing Medical Romances for nearly five years now, and also writes for Mills & Boon® Modern Extra™. She says it's the best of both worlds, because she gets to learn lots of new things when she's researching the background to a book: add a touch of passion, drama and danger, a new gorgeous hero every time, and it's the perfect job! Kate's always delighted to hear from readers, so do drop in to her website at www.katehardy.com

Recent titles by the same author:

THE FIREFIGHTER'S FIANCÉ
HIS HONOURABLE SURGEON*
HER HONOURABLE PLAYBOY*
HER CELEBRITY SURGEON*
THE CONSULTANT'S CHRISTMAS PROPOSAL

*Posh Docs

THEIR CHRISTMAS
DREAM COME TRUE

BY
KATE HARDY

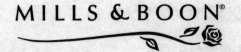

MILLS & BOON®

First published in Great Britain 2006
Harlequin Mills & Boon Limited,
Eton House, 18-24 Paradise Road, Richmond, Surrey TW9 1SR

© Pamela Brooks 2006

ISBN-13: 978 0 263 84765 9
ISBN-10: 0 263 84765 9

Set in Times Roman 10½ on 12¾ pt
03-1106-49591

Printed and bound in Spain
by Litografia Rosés, S.A., Barcelona

THEIR CHRISTMAS DREAM COME TRUE

CHAPTER ONE

SO THIS was it. Natalie's first day as a doctor—a pre-registration house officer, if you wanted to split hairs, but a brand-new doctor was still a doctor. Her hospital ID badge said DR NATALIE WILKINS. This was what she'd worked for. Hard. Against everyone's advice. And she'd finally made it. So what if she was six years older than the other house officers? The important thing was, she'd been offered a six months' post in the paediatric department of St Joseph's hospital.

Not the same hospital as Ethan—

Natalie cut the thought short before it could grab hold and choke her with remembered misery.

Paediatrics was probably the toughest option she could have chosen. Six years ago, she'd thought she'd never be able to walk onto a children's ward again. But she could do it and she *would* do it. Six months here, six months in emergency medicine, then back to paediatrics. Next move: senior house officer. Two years' further training and she'd be taking the paediatric specialist exams. And from there she'd make a real difference. Maybe stop other parents going through—

No. She wasn't going to think about that now. She had work to do.

She headed for the reception desk on the ward and introduced herself to the maternal-looking nurse in the dark blue uniform who was working through a stack of patient files. 'I was told to report here.'

Even though she'd tried to sound cool, calm and professional, some of her first-day nerves must have shown, because the nurse gave her a beaming smile. 'Hello, love. Welcome to Nightingale Ward. I'm Debbie Jacobs, the senior sister—I was off duty when you came for interview. You've got a few minutes until Lenox arrives, so let me show you where everything is.'

'Thanks.'

Fifteen minutes later, Natalie had a key to her own locker in the staffroom, knew where the parents' rooms and isolation cubicles were as well as the general bays, had gulped down her first cup of coffee on the ward, had been introduced to ten people whose names she was sure she'd never remember, and had started a ward round with Lenox Curtis, the consultant.

In at the deep end.

Doing observations, checking medication and treatment plans, venturing her opinion when it was asked for. Hesitantly, at first, but the more she got right, the more her confidence blossomed. By the end, she was able to reassure the anxious parents of a seven-month-old girl who'd been brought in with abdominal pain.

'Maia was always a colicky baby, but she seemed to be getting better. Then she started drawing her legs up again and screaming for two or three minutes.' The little girl's mother was shaking. 'She's been off her food the last day. And then I saw this red stuff in her nappy.'

'A bit like redcurrant jelly?' Natalie asked.

'Yes.'

Natalie examined the little girl gently. The baby's stomach was distended, and Natalie could feel a sausage-shaped mass, curved and concave to the umbilical cord. As Natalie gently pressed the mass, Maia lifted her legs and screamed again.

'All right, sweetheart.' Natalie soothed the baby gently, stroking her face and calming her down. She noted that the soft spot on the top of the baby's head had sunk a bit, showing that the little girl was dehydrated.

'What's wrong with her?' Maia's father asked.

'It's something called intussusception—it's where one segment of the bowel telescopes into another segment and constricts the blood supply. That's why you see the redcurrant-jelly-like stuff—it's a mixture of blood and mucus. But it's nothing either of you have done,' she reassured them both swiftly. 'It just happens. It might be that she has a polyp—a non-cancerous growth—that started it off. Quite a lot of children get intussusception before they're two, so we're very used to treating it here. I'm going to send her for an ultrasound in a minute so we can see exactly what we're looking at—it doesn't hurt and it's the same sort of scan you had when you were pregnant.'

Maia's father turned white. 'Is she going to have to have surgery?'

'Hopefully not. You've brought her in early, so we might be able to sort it out by an air enema—what we do is put a pipe in her bottom and blow air in to gently manoeuvre the bowel back to where it should be. If that doesn't work, we'll need to sort her bowel out surgically, but the good news is she's got an excellent chance of a full recovery.' She smiled at them. 'I'll book Maia in for an ultrasound now, and because she's a bit dehydrated I'm going to put her on a drip so we can get some fluids into her. In the meantime, to make her a bit more comfortable, I need to put a tube into her nose and down into her tummy—that will help get rid of any air that's built up.' It also drained the stomach contents, which made the procedures easier. 'I'll be able to give you a better idea of how we're going to treat her when I've seen the scan.'

'But she'll be OK?' Maia's mother asked.

'She's going to be fine,' Natalie promised. Had the problem been left a few weeks longer, gangrene might have set in, and the outcome would have been very different. But she was confident that this case would be absolutely fine.

And it felt good, so *good*, to help people. To make a difference to people's lives. To make things right again.

'So did you enjoy your first ward round here?' Lenox asked when they'd finished.

'I think so,' Natalie said with a smile. 'It was a bit nerve-racking to start with, but it got easier towards the end.'

He smiled back. 'You'll do fine. Give it a week and you'll feel as if you've been here for ever. And tomorrow you won't even be our newest recruit.'

'You've got another house officer starting?' Natalie asked, interested.

'Special registrar,' Lenox explained. 'We were lucky to poach him from London—he's quite a whiz. His name's Christopher Rodgers.'

Ice trickled down Natalie's spine. *Christopher Rodgers.*

No, it had to be a coincidence. Rodgers was a common enough surname, and Christopher was a popular first name. There was more than just one Christopher Rodgers in the world.

'Though it seems everyone calls him Kit,' Lenox added. *Kit?*

Most Christophers were known as Chris. Kit was the posh diminutive. A much, much less common diminutive.

Kit Rodgers.

From London.

No. It couldn't be him. Surely.

The Kit she'd known had been training as a surgeon, not as a paediatric specialist. Then again, Natalie had been a history teacher and she'd retrained. Kit might have done the same thing…for the same reasons.

Well, she'd deal with it tomorrow.

If she had to.

She managed to put Kit out of her mind when she took Maia for an ultrasound. The results showed the double ring she was expecting. 'Definitely intussusception.'

'Anything else?' Lenox asked.

She looked carefully at the scan. 'It doesn't look as if there's any perforation or significant ischaemia. So I'd say it would be safe to go ahead with the air enema.'

'Good call,' he said. 'Would you like me to talk you through it, or would you prefer to watch me do it?'

'I've seen one done before, though I haven't actually performed one,' she said. 'I'd like to try myself, if that's all right with you.'

'That's fine.' He smiled. 'I think you're going to be an asset to the team—you're prepared to try things rather than hang back. Good.'

He talked her through the procedure. As the pressure-regulated air gently pushed into the bowel, the bowel began to expand and the constricted part finally untelescoped.

'Bingo,' Lenox said with a smile. 'You've done it. Happy about managing the after-care?'

'Yes.'

'Good. You can go and talk to the parents on your own.'

She smiled at him, and went to see Maia's parents. 'You'll be pleased to know the procedure was a complete success, so Maia won't need to go for surgery. We're going to keep her in for a day or so, just to keep an eye on her and sort out her fluids, but she should be fine.'

'Oh, thank God,' Maia's mother said.

'Could she get it again?' Maia's father asked.

'It's extremely unlikely,' Natalie reassured them.

'Thank you so much, Dr Wilkins.'

Natalie smiled, and left them making a fuss over their little girl. So this was what being a doctor was all about. Making a difference. Helping.

She could almost understand why Kit had buried himself in his job.

Almost.

It was good to be home. Well, not quite home, Kit thought. He hadn't actually lived in Birmingham when he'd worked there before. He'd lived in Litchford-in-Arden, a little Warwickshire village halfway between Birmingham and Stratford-upon-Avon, in a picture-postcard cottage that overlooked the village green with its duck-pond and huge oak tree. Close to an ancient church where part of his heart would always lie.

When his world had fallen apart, Kit had fled to London. He'd wanted to lose himself in the anonymity of the city, avoid the pitying glances and the sympathy of people around him. It had worked for a while, but the busyness of the city had never really eased the ache in his heart. He'd never quite been able to block it out, no matter how many hours he worked or how hard he drove himself.

Now he was back. Near enough maybe to find some peace, but far enough away that people around him wouldn't know about the past. And, more to the point, they wouldn't offer him the pity he didn't want—didn't *need*. He was a paediatric specialist, and a good one, on track to becoming a consultant. He'd be good for St Joseph's, and St Joseph's would be good for him. Yes, this was going to work out just fine.

And everything *was* fine until he walked into the staffroom and saw the woman in a white coat talking to another woman in a sister's uniform. His heart missed a beat.

Tally.

Except it couldn't be. Tally was a teacher, not a doctor. And this woman had short, cropped hair instead of Tally's Pre-Raphaelite curls. She was thinner than Tally, too. No, he was just seeing things. Wishful thinking, maybe. And he needed to get his subconscious wishes back under control, right now. Stop seeing his ex-wife in every stranger's face. The past was the past and it was going to stay that way.

And then the woman looked up, saw him and every bit of colour leached from her face.

He wouldn't be surprised if he'd gone just as white. Because it really was her. It was the first time they'd met in five and a half years. 'Tally?' The name felt as if it had been ripped from him.

'Natalie,' she corrected. 'Hello, Kit.'

Her voice was like ice. A voice that had once been warm and soft, a voice that had once slurred his name in passion.

But that had been before Ethan.

'Do you two know each other?' the nurse she'd been talking to asked.

'We went to the same university,' Tally cut in quickly. 'We haven't seen each other in years.'

It was the truth. But very, very far from the whole truth. Obviously Tally didn't want to admit just how well they'd known each other.

Then again, Kit didn't exactly want the whole truth known either. Or the gossip and speculation that was bound to go with it.

Hell, hell, hell. If he'd had any idea that Tally had become a doctor—that she was working here—he would never have come to St Joseph's. He'd have stayed in London. Maybe even gone abroad for a while, got some experience in America or worked for Doctors Without Borders.

A quick glance at her ID badge told him that Tally was using her maiden name. Not that that meant anything. She might be married again now. Though he couldn't see a ring on her left hand, or a tell-tale band of paler skin on her ring finger. Maybe not married, then. Probably living with someone. Family was important to Natalie. She wouldn't be living on her own. She'd clearly moved on with her life.

Just like he had.

And he damped down the 'if only' before it had a chance to echo in his head.

He focused on the nurse and extended his hand. 'Kit Rodgers. Pleased to meet you. I'm the new boy.'

'And I'm Debbie Jacobs. Senior sister, for my sins.' The nurse smiled at him. 'Well, you've plenty in common with our Natalie, then. She's new, too—she started yesterday.' She gave them both a curious look. 'Since you know each other, you two must have a lot to catch up on.'

Natalie's reaction was clearly written on her face. *Not if I can help it.*

'We didn't really know each other that well,' Kit said coolly. Again, not the whole truth, but true enough. By the end, they'd been complete strangers. Living separate lives. And he'd wondered if he'd ever really known her.

'Natalie, maybe you can show Kit where everything is?'

'Um, yes. Sure.' And she smiled.

Oh, hell. He knew that smile. The bright one that pretended nothing was wrong—when, inside, everything was wrong. The one that spelled trouble with a capital T.

This was surreal. Natalie was showing Kit around the ward—and they were both acting as if they were polite strangers. Considering they'd known each other much more intimately, this was crazy.

'So you're a house officer. I didn't know you'd become a doctor. Your parents never said,' Kit remarked.

Natalie stared at him in shock. Her parents? Why would her parents have said anything to him about her change in career? 'You stayed in touch with them?'

He shrugged. 'Just Christmas and birthdays.'

Strange. She couldn't remember ever seeing a card from him on the mantelpiece. Or maybe her mum had kept it to one side when she had been around. Trying to save her daughter from more hurt. Seeing Kit's name in a card, maybe with another woman's name added after it.

And Natalie had to admit, it would've hurt. A lot. Even though, logically, she knew, of course, Kit had moved on. He was probably married by now. A man like Kit Rodgers wouldn't have stayed on his own for long. With cornflower blue eyes, dark hair and a killer smile, he was drop-dead gorgeous. Women adored him. Even when she'd been married to him, women had chased him. He'd never been short of offers, even though he'd always turned them down. Lack of fidelity wasn't one of his faults.

'You know your mum,' Kit continued. 'She always writes a lovely note in with a card.'

He sounded affectionate towards her parents. Though it wasn't so surprising. She knew he'd loved them—and they'd adored him. So had her younger sisters. Kit had the ability to charm just about anyone he met. Of course her parents would have stayed in touch with him.

Though Kit's parents hadn't stayed in touch with her. Also not surprising: they'd always been slightly wary of each other. Kit's family had always made her feel as if she wasn't quite good enough, as if a BA and a PCGE were somehow the second-class option, well beneath the notice of a family of doctors. She'd never really fitted in. Kit's parents and his three older brothers had all been medics, all high flyers. They'd seen her as a distraction, the person who'd stopped Kit achieving his full potential. She knew it wasn't true and she would have shrugged it off quite cheerfully, had it not been the fact they'd blamed her for Ethan.

Natalie pushed the thought back where it belonged—locked away with all the other feelings—and gave him a whistle-stop tour of the ward. 'This is the staffroom. Lockers here, kettle here, tea and coffee here, mugs in that cupboard, biscuits in the tin, milk in the fridge. Debbie has the kitty—and she's the one you tell if you notice we're running low on anything.' Out of the staffroom, back on to the ward. 'Nurses' station, patient board, so you know who's the nominated nurse, parents' phone, parents' room.'

Done and dusted.

'Thank you, Tally.'

'Natalie,' she corrected, annoyed at the amusement in his voice. So what if she'd rushed showing him round? Besides, she wasn't 'Tally' any more. To anyone.

She sneaked a glance at him. He'd barely changed in the last few years. A couple of grey hairs around his temples, a couple more lines on his face. But basically Kit Rodgers was the same. The epitome of tall, dark and handsome. Charming and easygoing with it, too—the female staff in the hospital would be falling at his feet in droves. So would the patients. And their parents. There wouldn't be any difficult cases on Nightingale Ward when Kit Rodgers was around: that easy-going smile was too infectious. Men would identify with him and women would fall for him. He'd manage to get a good response from even the stroppiest parent.

Except maybe from her.

She knew better. She'd keep things cool and professional between them.

He wasn't wearing a wedding ring, she noticed. Not that that meant anything. He hadn't worn one before either. Well, she wasn't going to ask him if he was married. And she definitely wasn't going to ask the question that usually went with that one. She wasn't interested.

Ha. Who was she trying to kid? More like, she wasn't sure she could handle the answer.

'I, um, need to get ready for the ward round,' she said. 'Catch you later.' As in preferably much later. Better still, as in not at all. 'Lenox's office is just there.'

And she walked away, quickly, while she still could.

CHAPTER TWO

NATALIE managed to avoid Kit for most of the morning, and at lunchtime she had the unimpeachable excuse of needing to get her shoes reheeled during her lunch-break. But in the afternoon they were both rostered to the outpatient clinic. Thrown together. No respite.

Well, she could deal with this. Kit was just another doctor. A colleague. She'd keep him neatly pigeonholed there.

'So, would this be your first clinic since you qualified?' Kit asked as they headed to the outpatients area.

'Yes,' she admitted.

'OK. You lead. I'll be here for back-up, if you need me.'

Being supportive? *Kit?* Well. Maybe he'd grown up in the last six years. He was thirty now, after all. And he was the more experienced doctor out of the two of them. Several rungs higher than she was. He was just doing what she'd do if the positions were reversed. Giving a junior doctor a chance to gain experience, with a safety net if it was needed.

But this *was* her first proper clinic. And he wanted her to lead. Take responsibility. 'What if I miss something?' she asked.

He shrugged. 'Then I'll bring it up in conversation

with the parents. But I won't tear you off a strip in front of them or make you look incompetent, if that's what you're thinking.'

She felt her skin heat. 'I wasn't sniping at you. What I meant was, I might get something wrong, put a patient at risk.' She was worried that she wasn't totally ready for this, that maybe in her first clinic she should take a supportive role rather than a lead. 'Are you going to take everything I say personally, for goodness' sake?'

He raked a hand through his hair. 'No. Sorry.'

It had probably been gut reaction. She supposed it must be just as difficult for him, having to work with her and ignore their history. And there had been plenty of sniping in their last few months together. Mainly by her—because Kit hadn't been there often enough and the frustration and misery had made her temper short.

'You'll be fine in clinic. You're qualified, so you obviously know your stuff. If it's something with a tricky diagnosis, something that could easily be mistaken for a different condition, I'll be here to take a look. I'll give a second opinion when you ask for it, and I'll back you up,' Kit said.

Just what she needed to hear. And if only he'd been that supportive all those years ago, when she'd really needed him. Someone she could have leaned on when her strength had deserted her.

But you couldn't change the past. Mentally, Natalie slammed the door on it and locked the key.

The first parent on their list was Ella Byford. She was reading a story to two rather grubby children who seemed to be squabbling about who was going to get the best place on her lap, while rubbing her back in the way that most heavily pregnant women did.

Something Natalie had once—

No. She clenched her teeth hard, just once, to relieve the tension, then reminded herself to keep her personal life out of this. She was a doctor. A paediatrician in training. This was her job. And she was going to do it well. She pinned a smile on her face. 'Hello, Mrs Byford. I'm Natalie Wilkins and this is Kit Rodgers. We're holding the paediatric clinic today. What can we do for you?'

'It's Charlene. Jayden's all right, he's doing fine.' Ella waved a dismissive hand towards her son. 'But Charlene's so *skinny*. She's not doing as well as she should. She's always been small for dates, but she's getting worse.' Ella bit her lip. 'I went to see my GP about her, and he sent me here.'

'Let's have a look at her,' Natalie said. She knelt on the floor so she was nearer to the little girl's height. 'Hello, Charlene.'

''Lo.' The little girl looked at her and scowled.

OK, she could do this. Thin, small for dates. The little girl was quite pale—perhaps she just didn't get to play outside very much, or her mum was rigorous with a high protection factor suncream. Or maybe it was anaemic pallor. Natalie needed to check for icterus—or a yellowish colour—too. Starting with the child's fingernails, palms, mucous membranes of the mouth and the conjunctiva. The conjunctiva would be the tricky part—children hated having their eyes fussed with.

'Can you open your mouth for me and say "a-ah"?' she asked.

'A-ah.' It lasted all of half a second, but it was enough to show Natalie that there was slight pallor in Charlene's mouth but no icterus. It didn't look as if there were any ulcers, but if Natalie saw any other sinister signs in the rest of the examination she'd try for a second look.

'And can I look at your hands now?'

Charlene scowled at her and tried to climb back on her mother's lap.

'Charlene, be nice for the doctor,' Ella admonished her.

'It's not fair. I want to sit on your lap. He *always* does.' Charlene shoved at her brother, who promptly fell off Ella's lap and started howling.

Kit stepped in smoothly. 'Hey. How about I read you a story, Jayden, while the doctor talks to your mum and your sister?' He took two shiny stickers from his pocket. 'And if you can both sit really still while the doctor's talking— and while the doctor's looking at you, Charlene—you can both have a special sticker.'

Why hadn't *she* thought of that? Natalie wondered. And as a distraction technique it clearly worked, because Charlene immediately nodded, climbed onto her mother's lap and sat still, while Jayden plonked himself on Kit's lap so he could see the pictures in the story book. Ella, who'd looked close to tears, suddenly relaxed.

Teamwork. Good teamwork. And Natalie wasn't going to let herself think about the fact that Kit was reading a story to a little boy.

'OK, Charlene. Shall we see if your hands are bigger than mine?'

'Don't be silly. They'll be smaller.'

'Bet they're not,' Natalie said, putting her own hands behind her back.

Charlene giggled. 'They are.'

'Show me, then.'

To Natalie's relief, when she brought her hands round

again, Charlene splayed her palms and pressed them against Natalie's.

'Side by side now. Palm up,' Natalie said.

The little girl, clearly thinking it was a game, did as she asked. Her palms were definitely pale, though at least there was no sign of yellowness.

'And the back, to see if you have princess nails?'

'You haven't got princess nails. They're not glittery,' Charlene said.

Natalie was glad that Charlene's weren't either: it gave her the chance to notice that the little girl's fingernails were concave.

'Can I look at your tummy now?'

'Can I look at yours?' Charlene asked.

'Not this time,' Natalie said with a smile. She definitely wasn't baring any flesh in front of Kit. 'But if you want to play doctors while I talk to your mummy, you can look at a doll's tummy and see what you can hear through my stethoscope.'

Charlene wriggled a bit, but submitted to an examination. Natalie palpated her abdomen gently. She didn't think there was a problem with the spleen, but maybe she should ask Kit for a second opinion. No sign of petechiae, reddish-purple pinhead spots, which would lead to a more sinister diagnosis. And, she was pleased to note, there were no signs of enlarged lymph nodes in Charlene's neck.

As soon as she'd finished, Charlene was wriggling around on Ella's lap again, and Ella pressed one fist into her lower back for support. Natalie gave Ella a sympathetic smile. It must be hard, dealing with small children when you were heavily pregnant and tired.

'She's a handful for such a little scrap,' Ella said, looking embarrassed.

Oh, no. That hadn't been what she'd intended at all. Or maybe Ella was just used to being defensive about her little girl. 'Lively, the medical term is,' Natalie said with a smile. 'How's she eating?'

Ella grimaced. 'She's picky. She won't eat any vegetables—she just throws them on the floor—and she doesn't like anything with meat in it, even if I try to hide it. But I can get her to eat potatoes and eggs, and she drinks milk and fruit juice.'

It was nowhere near a balanced diet, and Ella was clearly aware of it—distressed about it, too, so Natalie decided to take the gentle approach. 'Kids are notorious for that—one day they'll eat something, and the next they won't touch it,' she said reassuringly. 'How about you take me through right from the start, from when she was first born?' She could already see that Charlene had had a low birthweight, something that could predispose her to anaemia. 'Did she have any jaundice afterwards?'

'She was a bit yellow, but the midwife said it was normal.'

Natalie nodded. 'Most babies have it to some extent.' Though Ethan hadn't. He'd been a perfect seven and a half pounds. No problems at all. Prolonged jaundice in the newborn could suggest congenital anaemia. 'How long did it last?'

'A week or so.'

'How was she feeding?'

'I breastfed her for about a week.' Ella grimaced. 'I tried so hard, but I just couldn't manage it. My husband works long hours and it was too much for me. I got so tired—she seemed to be constantly attached to me, just taking little bits here and there, and I never got a break. And I was so sore.'

No support at home, and a husband who wasn't there more often than not. Yeah, Natalie could empathise with that one. Really empathise. She couldn't help glancing at Kit—and looked away again the second she met his cornflower-blue gaze. She just hoped she wasn't blushing. Hell. This was meant to be about her patient, not about her and Kit.

'So I switched her to formula milk,' Ella continued.

And felt she'd failed as a result. It was very clear in Ella's face—guilt, worry that she'd done the wrong thing, that she'd given up at the first hurdle without really trying. 'Hey, that's fine,' Natalie said. 'I know you read everywhere that breast is best, but you have to do what works for you as a family. Don't listen to anyone who tries to make you feel bad or says you did the wrong thing. How did she take to formula milk?'

'OK. I started putting a bit of rice in to her milk when she was two months old, to help her sleep a bit better and stop her being hungry in the night.'

Ouch. That sounded as if Ella had been desperate and had taken advice from the older generation—probably someone who'd gone on and on and on when Ella had been tired, about how Ella had been a baby who had always woken in the night and a bit of rice had never hurt her. Nowadays, the recommendation was to wait until at least four months before weaning.

Careful not to pass judgment, Natalie asked, 'What happened then?'

'She slept through, but she dropped a bit of weight then, and when she was three months the health visitor said maybe we'd be better off with a soya-based formula.' Ella bit her lip. 'But her charts still kept doing down.'

'Do you have the charts with you, by any chance?' Natalie asked.

'Oh, yes. I've got her red book.' Ella dug in her handbag and eventually brought out a slightly dog-eared book with a C written neatly on the front. Natalie flicked to the charts. At birth, Charlene's weight had been a little below average, on the fortieth centile: meaning that sixty per cent of babies at the same age would be heavier than she was. By three months, Charlene had dropped to the tenth centile, from six to twelve months her weight was on the third centile, and the measurement the paediatric nurse had done a few minutes before showed she'd dropped below even that. Charlene's height, too, was below average, on the twenty-fifth centile. But Ella had clearly taken care to have her daughter's height and weight measured regularly, and as Natalie flicked through the book she noticed that all the immunisations were up to date.

'She's a bit of a tomboy,' Ella said apologetically as Charlene stopped fidgeting, wriggled off her lap and headed straight for the toybox, emptying the entire contents out. 'I've stopped trying to keep her clean all day. She starts out with fresh clothes, but if I changed her every time she gets grubby…well. I'd never have the washing machine off. So I just put her in the bath every night and give her a good wash.' She bit her lip. 'I was wondering if she had—' her voice lowered in obvious embarrassment '—worms, or something. If that's why she's skinny. Can you do an X-ray or something to check?'

'An X-ray's probably not going to be very helpful right now,' Natalie said gently, 'and we don't want to expose Charlene to radiation if we don't really have to. As for the other problem—' she'd picked up on how awkward Ella clearly felt '—you'd be surprised at just how common it is. Kids pick them up really easily. Does she talk about itching at all? Or do you see her scratching her bottom?'

'Well, no,' Ella admitted.

'It's unlikely to be worms, then,' Natalie reassured her. 'Though if you really want to be sure, when she's asleep tonight, take a torch and shine it on her bottom. If you see anything white and wriggling, you'll need to nip into the chemist and get some worming treatment—and do the whole family, not just Charlene. You'll also need to keep her nails really short and get a soft nailbrush to keep them clean. What happens with worms is that a child scratches their bottom and some tiny eggs—so small you can't see them—can end up beneath their nails. Kids that age normally have their hands in their mouth half the time so the eggs come out again, and the whole cycle starts again. It's not anything you've done, so don't worry.' She paused. 'Does Charlene eat anything odd?' She was pretty sure the problem was chronic iron deficiency, and pica—eating abnormal things that weren't food, such as coal—often went with it.

Ella shook her head. 'I try and keep her off chips but sometimes it's just easier to give in. At least then I know she's eaten something.'

'What about the toilet? Is she dry at night?'

'Been out of nappies for ages. Just as well—Jayden isn't, and I don't think I could cope with three of them in nappies,' Ella admitted.

Natalie smiled at her. 'That'd be quite a tough call. Tell me, is anyone else in the family very light, or quite short?'

Ella shrugged. 'We're all pretty average, really.'

Not a genetic thing, then. The next thing to rule out was the possibility of a developmental disorder. She doubted it, because she'd heard for herself that Charlene's speech was clear and her words were average for a three-year-old. 'Is there anything you've noticed about the way she behaves, or the way she speaks?'

Ella shook her head. 'She's just a bit lively and a bit of a tomboy.' She frowned. 'You don't think she has that thing where she'll have to go on Ritalin, do you?'

'ADHD? No,' Natalie said, shaking her head. 'I think it's all to do with her being a fussy eater. It means she isn't getting a balanced diet, and her iron stores are too low.' Plus she'd been weaned too early. 'She's probably anaemic and iron deficient. It's not serious,' she reassured Ella, 'and I can give you some iron supplements to help that. She'll need to take them for about three months. But I'll also refer you to a dietician, so she can help you with a few coping strategies to persuade Charlene to eat some meat and a few more vegetables.'

'I do *try*,' Ella said.

'Of course you do. But sometimes you can do with a helping hand,' Natalie said. 'Being a parent's one of the hardest jobs on earth.' Though not being a parent could sometimes be even harder. She shook herself. 'I'd like to take a blood sample and a wee sample, so I can check the chemicals in Charlene's blood and that her kidneys and liver are working as they should be. I'll give you a follow-up appointment for a fortnight's time so I can check her weight and height and how she's responding to treatment.' She paused. 'When are you due?'

'In a month, though Jayden was three weeks early and this one might be the same.'

'Maybe Charlene's dad can bring her in?' Natalie suggested.

'He's busy at work,' Ella said swiftly. 'And he never remembers appointments anyway.'

Unsupportive husband. Oh, Natalie knew all about that.

The sympathy must have shown on her face, because Ella added, 'But I'll try.' With the same defensive note Natalie remembered in her own voice when she'd been the one making excuses.

Natalie took the blood sample—following it up immediately with one of Kit's stickers—and talked Ella through taking the urine sample, then directed her to the reception area to book the next appointment.

'What are you going to order?' Kit asked as Natalie labelled the sample.

'Full blood count, differential, electrolytes, calcium, phosphate, magnesium, iron, ferritin, folate, albumin and total protein, plus renal and liver function.'

He smiled. 'Perfect.'

'I didn't miss anything, then?'

He spread his hands. 'Maybe the involvement of Social Services?'

Natalie stared at him. 'You must be joking. You don't seriously think this is abuse by neglect, do you?'

'Convince me,' Kit said, his voice and face completely neutral so she couldn't even guess what he was thinking.

'In a month's time, Ella Byford will have a newborn, a toddler and an under-four. Her partner clearly doesn't pull his weight with the kids and she's making excuses for him—sure, she's having trouble coping right now and she needs a bit of support, but it's definitely not neglect. Firstly, she's the one who went to her GP because she was worried—it wasn't the health visitor or GP prompting the appointment. Secondly, Charlene's vaccinations are all up to date—which they wouldn't be if she was being neglected. And, thirdly, Ella's been meticulous about recording weight measurements. It's not just the health visitor or GP's measurements on the chart—some of the entries had Ella's initials against them. This isn't a mum who's neglecting her kids, it's a mum who's having a rough time and needs support she isn't getting from her partner.'

The words echoed between them and she couldn't meet his eyes.

But Kit's voice was perfectly level as he said, 'Good call. I agree with your assessment. But,' he added, 'remember that you're dealing with patients. You need to keep your personal feelings out of it.'

The rebuke stung, the more so because she knew it was merited. She *was* bringing her personal feelings into it, and it was the wrong thing to do.

'I'll bear it in mind,' she said, matching the coolness of his tone.

'Good. Next patient, I think.'

They got through the rest of the clinic, and Kit surprised her at the end by saying, 'You did well.'

'Thank you.' Though she didn't meet his eyes.

He sighed. 'Tal—'

'Natalie,' she corrected swiftly. 'My name is Natalie.'

'Natalie.' He gritted his teeth. 'Look, we're going to have to work together for a while. Six months, at least. So maybe we should just… I dunno. Clear the air between us.'

She thought not. Some things couldn't be cleared. Ever.

'We're both due a break. Let's go and have a coffee,' he said.

She didn't want to. How could she possibly sit across the table from Kit and pretend everything was all right? Because it wasn't all right. Never would be.

He sighed. 'Natalie, if we leave this, it's just going to get worse. We need to set some ground rules. And it won't kill you to sit at a table with me and drink coffee.' His mouth gave the tiniest quirk. 'Though I'd appreciate it if you drank it rather than threw it at me.'

'Since when did you learn to read minds?'

'It's written all over your face,' he said wryly.

At the canteen, she refused to let him pay for her cappuccino, and he didn't press the point. He still drank black coffee, she noticed—obviously he hadn't broken the habit from his student days. Or his habit of snacking on chocolate: he'd bought a brownie with his coffee.

'So what made you become a doctor?' he asked when he'd taken his first sip of coffee.

She exhaled sharply. 'What do you think?'

'The same reason I switched from surgery to paediatrics,' he said softly. 'It won't change the past. But I might be able to help someone in the future. Stop them going through…'

He left the words unsaid, but she knew exactly what Kit was thinking. He could have been speaking for her. His voice had even held that same hopeless yearning when he'd said it—knowing he couldn't change the past, but wanting to anyway. And wanting other people not to have to go through what they'd been through.

Natalie willed the tears to stay back. She'd cried all she was ever going to cry over Kit Rodgers. No more.

'You've done well,' Kit said. 'Lenox was telling me how you were the star student of your year.'

Natalie shrugged. 'I studied hard.' And it hadn't been completely new ground. She could remember some of it from the time when she'd helped Kit revise for his finals.

Tally really wasn't going to make this easy. Not that he could blame her. He'd let her down when she'd needed him most.

But seeing her again, like this... It made him realise how much he'd missed her. How empty his life had been without her. And why he hadn't bothered dating very often, let alone having a serious relationship. He'd always claimed once bitten, twice shy, and all that, but now he had to admit there was a little more to it than that.

Simply, nobody had ever been able to match up to Tally.

He understood why she hated him. He'd hated her, too, at one point. Especially the day she'd walked out on him and left him that bloody note saying she wanted a divorce and her solicitor would be in touch. But he'd missed her. Missed the way she'd said his name. Missed her smile, missed her quick wit, missed her touch.

Part of him thought that everything would be all right if he could just touch her, hold her, say he was sorry and ask her to wipe the slate clean.

But he knew that slate could never be wiped clean. And touching her was out of the question. There was a brick wall twenty feet high between them, with an enormous ditch either side filled with barbed wire.

Ah, hell. They were supposed to be clearing the air between them—his idea—and now he was tongue-tied. He made an effort. 'Where are you living now?'

'Birmingham.'

She wasn't giving a millimetre—wouldn't even tell him where she lived. Birmingham was a city of almost a million people, so she could be living just about anywhere within a radius of twenty miles of St Joseph's.

'Me, too. I'm renting,' he said.

No response—no 'Me, too' or 'I'm in the middle of buying a flat'. She was freezing him out. Frustration made him sharp. 'I thought about seeing if there was anywhere to rent in Litchford-in-Arden,' he said, watching her closely.

She flinched at the name of the village.

Good. So she wasn't entirely frozen, then.

'I drove through the village yesterday.' He waited a beat. 'Past our house.'

She still said nothing, but he noticed she was gripping her coffee-mug and her knuckles were white. She was clearly trying not to react, but he wasn't going to let her do it. He'd get over the barrier between them, even if he had to make her crack first. He'd *make* her talk to him.

'There was a…'

But there was a lump in his throat blocking the words. He couldn't say it. It hurt too much, and at the realisation his anger died. What was the point of this? It was hurting both of them, and it wasn't going to solve a thing.

'A child. About six years old. Playing in the garden. I know,' Tally said, her voice shaky as she continued what he'd been about to say. 'I…went back, too. A couple of weeks ago. The woman was weeding the garden.' Her breath hitched. 'She was pregnant.'

Kit could remember Tally, pregnant, weeding their garden. Tending her flowers—she'd made it a proper cottage garden with hollyhocks and lavender and love-in-a-mist. To see another woman doing the same thing, in *their* garden—pregnant, with a child around six years old cycling round the garden—must have burned like acid in her soul.

He'd found it hard enough to handle, seeing someone else living their dreams. For Tally, it must have been so much worse. And he hated the fact that he hadn't been there to hold her, comfort her when she'd discovered it.

But he was here now. He could do something now. He reached out and took her free hand. Squeezed it gently. 'It should have been us, Tally,' he said quietly. 'It should have been us.'

She wrenched her hand away. 'But it isn't. Wasn't. We can't change the past, Kit. We can't go back. Someone else lives there now.'

In their house. The house where they'd made love. The house where they'd made a baby.

The house where their dreams had died. Where their love had been reduced to solicitors' letters. Cold legal words. The end of everything.

'We have to work together,' Tally said, 'but that's as far as it goes. I'm sure we're both mature enough to be civil to each other.'

'Of course.'

A muscle flickered in her jaw. 'I don't think there's anything left to say. We've both moved on.'

Had they? 'Are you married?'

'That's not relevant.'

Which told him nothing. And she clearly didn't want to know whether he was or not, because she didn't ask. He really, really should let this go.

So why couldn't he?

'Tal— Natalie,' he corrected himself swiftly, 'It doesn't have to be like this.'

She pushed her chair back. 'Let's just agree to disagree, hmm?'

And then she was walking away from him.

Again.

And he was left with the feeling that he'd just made things a hell of a lot worse.

CHAPTER THREE

FOR the next couple of days, Natalie successfully continued to avoid Kit. But then they were rostered together again, this time on the paediatric assessment unit.

'Dr Wilkins, I take it this is your first PAU?' Kit asked.

On an intellectual level, she knew the formality was the right way to go—keeping a professional distance between them would be a good thing—but, oh, it stung. Had they really been reduced to this, to titles and surnames, after everything they'd shared? 'Correct, Dr Rodgers,' she responded, equally coolly.

'Do you want to do this as a teaching session, or would you like to lead and I'll back you up?'

He was giving her the choice. Not much of one. Either way, they had to work together. Closely. And she was finding it harder than she'd expected. Every time she glanced up at him she remembered other places, other times, when she'd caught his eye and seen a different expression there. Blue eyes filled with love and laughter. A lazy smile that had promised her some very personal attention once they were alone.

And now he was this cool, remote stranger. Just like he'd

been at the end of their marriage. Reacting to nothing and nobody. Closed off.

'PAU's where we get the urgent referrals, isn't it?' she asked.

'Yes.'

Where her diagnoses really could mean life or death. She took a deep breath. 'Right.' Was she ready for this?

'Or we could lead on alternate cases. Do it together,' Kit added.

His tone of voice on the last word made her look at him. The expression in his eyes was quickly masked, but she'd seen something there. Something that surprised her. Regret, wishing things could have been different?

She pushed it to the back of her mind. Of course not. She was just wishing for something that wasn't there. Kit had shut her out six years ago, and he wasn't about to invite her back into his life now.

They'd both moved on.

Well, *he* had.

'OK.'

'Want me to take the first one?' he asked.

'Whatever you think best, Dr Rodgers,' she said, her voice completely without expression.

'In that case,' Kit said, 'I'm throwing you in at the deep end. You go first.'

Oh, Lord. She hadn't been expecting that. But if that was the way he wanted to play it, she'd show him she could do it—that she didn't need his help.

Their first case was a two-year-old with a fever and a rash. Ross Morley's eyes were red, as if he had conjunctivitis, although there didn't appear to be any discharge. 'He's had a temperature for a couple of days but he seems to be getting worse,' Mrs Morley said, twisting her hands together. 'His hands and feet look a bit red and I'm sure they're not normally as puffy as this. And then I saw this rash…'

'And you're worried that it's meningitis?' Natalie guessed.

Mrs Morley dragged in a breath. 'Don't let it be that. He's my only one. Please, don't let it be that.'

'Rashes can be scary,' Natalie said gently, 'but there are lots of things that can cause a rash like this.' Gently, she stretched the little boy's skin over the spotty area. 'The spots have faded, see? So it's unlikely to be meningitis—though you've done absolutely the right thing to bring him here,' she reassured Mrs Morley. 'If it had been meningitis, he could have become seriously ill extremely quickly. Has he been immunised against measles?'

'Yes. He had the MMR at fifteen months.'

'It's unlikely to be rubella or measles, then.' Natalie swiftly took the little boy's temperature with the ear thermometer—definitely raised. She continued examining him and noted that the lymph nodes in his neck were swollen. 'It could be glandular fever—what we call infectious mononucleosis—or this could be his body's reaction to a virus, most likely an echovirus.' She swallowed hard. 'Or Coxsackie virus.'

She couldn't help glancing at Kit. Saw her own pain echoed in his eyes. And she had to look away and clamp her teeth together so the sob would stay back. Coxsackie B. The tiny, invisible virus that had smashed her life into equally tiny pieces.

She turned back to the little boy and finished her examination. 'His skin's starting to peel at the fingertips.'

'He doesn't suck his thumb or anything,' Mrs Morley said. 'Never has.'

'I think Ross has Kawasaki disease,' Natalie said. 'Peeling skin's one of the signs, plus he has the rash, the redness and slight swelling in his hands, his eyes are red, his lips are dry and cracked, and he has a fever.' Kawasaki disease tended to be diagnosed clinically rather than through blood tests, and Ross Morley's case ticked all the boxes. She glanced at Kit for confirmation.

He nodded, and mouthed, 'Good call.'

She damped down the feeling of pleasure. She was doing this to help people, not to prove something to Kit.

'So what happens now?' Mrs Morley asked.

'We're going to admit him to the ward,' Natalie said. 'The good news is we can treat the disease. We'll give him aspirin and a drip with immunoglobulin drugs to fight the disease. Over the next few days, the fever and the swollen glands in his neck will go down and the rash will disappear, but Ross's eyes will still look a bit red and sore and the skin's going to continue peeling around his fingers, toes and the nappy area. He might feel some pain in his joints and you'll probably find he's a bit irritable, but the good news is that you'll be able to take him home next week and all the symptoms will gradually disappear. It'll take him another three weeks or so after that before he's completely over it, though.'

'Will there be any complications?'

Possibly myocarditis—inflammation of the heart muscle—but although Natalie's mouth opened, the words just wouldn't come out. Couldn't. The lump in her throat was too big.

'There can be complications with Kawasaki disease,' Kit said softly. 'Some children have arthritis afterwards, and some develop heart problems, but we'll send him for a follow-up echo to make sure—that's an ultrasound scan of the heart and it won't hurt at all, plus you can be with him while it's being done.'

Mrs Morley swallowed hard. 'Could he die?' she whispered.

'Most children make a full recovery,' Kit reassured her.

Most children. But myocarditis could be deadly. Sometimes there weren't even any symptoms. In very small children it was difficult to tell the problem—they couldn't tell you if they had chest pain, were tired or had palpitations. You just noticed the difficulty in breathing, which could be caused by just about any of the viruses causing a cough or cold in a little one. The over-fast heartbeat could only be picked up by monitoring. And the average person in the street wouldn't even know what S1 and S4 were, let alone that S1—the first heart sound, when the mitral and tricuspid valves closed—was soft if there was myocarditis, and S4— the fourth heart sound—made a galloping noise, like 'Tennessee', when tachycardia was involved. And then the heart stopped pumping efficiently. Failed. And finally stopped.

Just as Ethan's had. And all she'd been able to do had been to hold her little boy in her arms as his heart had finally given out and the life had seeped from his body. Natalie clenched her fists hard, willing herself to stay strong.

Though she was sure that Kit was thinking of Ethan, too. Especially because she noticed the tiniest wobble in his voice when he added, 'We'll get Ross booked onto the ward, Mrs Morley, and one of the nurses will take you up and help you settle him in.'

'Can I—can I ring my husband? He's at work. I was just so worried about Ross this morning, I couldn't wait for him to get home.'

Oh, yes. Natalie had been there, too. So sure that something was wrong, she hadn't waited for Kit. She'd left a message for him at work and taken Ethan to the emergency department. A mother's instinct was usually right: it was one of the things she'd been taught at med school. Parents knew when something was wrong with their children—they couldn't always put their finger on it, and the words 'he's just not right' were usually justified, on examining the child.

'No problem,' Kit said. 'I'll get our nurse to show you where the phone is. There's a special phone on our ward, too, which we keep as the parents' phone—you can give the number out if people want to ring you for an update, and you don't have to worry about blocking the ward's main line.'

When they handed Mrs Morley and Ross over to the liaison nurse, Kit turned to Natalie. 'Are you OK?'

'Sure,' she lied. 'Why shouldn't I be?' Though she could hear the cracks in her own voice. Ha. At least he wasn't bawling her out for not doing her job properly. He could have picked her up on the fact that she hadn't told Mrs Morley what the complications were. But he clearly understood how hard she found it to say the words. How she could barely breathe—it felt as if someone had put her whole body in a vice and was slowly, slowly squeezing it.

'If you want to take five minutes, have a glass of water or what have you, that's fine,' Kit said.

But that would be showing weakness. As good as saying that she couldn't cope with her job. And she *could*. It had just caught her unawares this time. Next time she'd handle it better. 'No, I'm fine,' she said tightly. 'I'm doing my job. I don't need mollycoddling.'

Perhaps she was being a little bloody-minded. But it jarred that Kit was trying to soften things for her now.

When she'd needed his support, six years ago, he hadn't been there.

'If you're sure.'

She couldn't stand him being so nice to her. Kindness wasn't what she wanted from Kit.

Though she wasn't going to think about what she did want from him.

'Tally. *Natalie*,' he corrected himself quickly, 'paediatrics is a tough option. Especially at this time of year. You're going to come across cases that remind you. Cases that have parallels. And some days you'll find it harder to deal with than others.'

Meaning that he did, too? She'd noticed that he hadn't actually said Ethan's name aloud. Would the word choke him, too?

Kit laid his hand on her shoulder. Squeezed it, giving the lightest of pressure. 'Natalie, if you need—'

No. She didn't need anything from Kit. 'We have a full list. Let's move on,' she cut in quickly. If he offered her a shoulder to cry on now, nearly six years too late, she couldn't bear it. She shrugged his hand off her shoulder, too—a white coat and her sweater weren't enough of a barrier between them. Right now she couldn't cope with feeling the warmth of his touch.

His voice cooled noticeably. 'Of course, Dr Wilkins.'

Somehow she got through the rest of the afternoon. But the more she saw of Kit working—the way he was able to soothe the most fretful child—the more she realised how good he was with kids. They responded to him, to his strength and calmness, someone who was clearly going to take the pain away and make them feel better.

He didn't rush through diagnoses either. He'd read a story if it was needed, or start telling a series of truly terrible jokes—jokes she'd had no idea he even knew—and made a game out of examinations. Let children listen to his heartbeat through his stethoscope. Took time to calm the worries of parents. Explained exactly what he was doing in terms the parents would understand, without frightening the child.

And she couldn't help thinking what a great dad he would have made. How he would have been with his own children, dealing with tantrums and tears without letting them fray his temper. He'd still have kept his fun side, too, flying kites and racing round on a bicycle and playing boisterous games with them.

What a waste. What a bloody, bloody *waste*.

Or was it? Did Kit have another family now? Another son to replace the one he'd lost? A daughter, perhaps, one who looked like his new wife?

Natalie wasn't sure what was worse: thinking about the dad he might have been, or thinking about the dad he might be now—to another woman's children, not hers.

It broke her up inside, though she managed to keep a cool front. Even had coffee with him after their PAU stint, although neither of them spoke much and they kept the topics strictly neutral. Work. Safe areas.

And then she had two blessed days off. Two days when she wasn't going to think of Kit at all. And by Monday, when she was on duty again, she'd be back in full control of her feelings.

'What a waste,' Fran sighed as she filled the kettle in the staffroom. 'He's so gorgeous, too.'

'Waste?' Natalie asked, frowning. What was Fran on about?

Ruth, the other nurse in the room, sighed dramatically. 'Tall, dark and handsome. Drop-dead gorgeous, in fact— the sort who makes your knees go wobbly every time he smiles. And he's a thoroughly nice bloke, too—not one of these who knows how gorgeous he is and expects every female he meets to worship him. He's *lovely*. He takes the time to explain things to parents—and to students. He's not one of these know-it-all doctors who think they're God and nurses don't have a brain cell to rub between them. He actually shows respect for the nursing staff. And he's gay,' she explained, looking equally disgruntled.

Natalie really wasn't following the conversation. 'Who is?'

Fran rolled her eyes. 'Kit, of course. Our new registrar. He's been here a week now. And you've been working with him in clinics and on ward rounds, so don't say you haven't noticed.'

Natalie blinked. 'That he's gay?'

'No, that he's gorgeous. I mean—tall, dark and handsome doesn't even begin to describe him. He's beautiful. And those eyes! Oh-h-h.' Ruth shook her head. 'You're too focused on your work, Natalie. You really need to chill out. Get out more.'

'Get a life. Yeah, I know,' Natalie said, forcing a smile to her face. There had been a time when she'd partied with the best of them. Before her marriage had crumbled into dust. Since then, she'd preferred a quiet life.

'It's such a waste,' Fran said again. 'You know, I can just imagine what it'd be like to be kissed by him. That beautiful mouth, doing all sorts of lovely things…' She gave a blissful shiver. 'Ooh.'

Natalie didn't need to imagine. She knew exactly what it was like to be kissed by him. How Kit's lips could elicit a response from hers. How his mouth could move from teasing to passion within a second, as heat flared between them. How his mouth had taken her to paradise and back.

She gritted her teeth, trying to push the memories back where they belonged—in the past. She and Kit were over. *Over.* Remembering stuff like this was pointless.

'I've got a friend who worked in his last hospital,' Fran continued. 'The nurses were falling over themselves to ask him out. He'd go on most of the staff nights out—he was always a good sport—but he never actually dated anyone. Turned down every single offer.' She looked thoughtful. 'Gina from the emergency department asked him out for a drink the other night. He turned her down—and considering Gina only has to click her fingers and men come running, panting…'

Kit didn't date? But… Natalie damped down the little flicker of hope. No. Absolutely not. She didn't want to start thinking about the reasons why Kit didn't date. Or her own reaction to the news that maybe, just maybe, Kit was still single, too.

If she told them she knew he wasn't gay, she'd have to explain. Which she didn't want to do. But she didn't want them getting the wrong idea about Kit either. 'Maybe he's just concentrating on his career.'

'The way you do, you mean? No, I'm pretty sure it's not that.' Fran shook her head mournfully. 'And it's not because he's an adoring husband because he's not married, either.'

Ruth nodded. 'I reckon he's just not interested in women. I mean, he notices things like shoes.'

'She's right, you know,' Fran said with a sigh. 'Only gay men notice things like shoes, don't they? Straight men don't think about what you're wearing, they think about how to get it off you.'

Natalie couldn't help smiling, but inside she ached. Of course Kit noticed shoes: once upon a time, Natalie had been a major shoe fiend and hadn't been able to pass a shoe shop without drooling over high heels in outrageous colours. Kit had bought them for her, even when they hadn't really been able to afford it.

And the day she'd discovered she was pregnant, she'd bought a tiny pair of white satin pram shoes. Had wrapped them up and given them to him. And when he'd worked it out, he'd picked her up and spun her round and—

'Hello? Earth to Natalie?' Fran said, waving one hand in front of her face and proffering a mug of coffee with the other.

She took the coffee with a rueful smile. 'Thanks, Fran. Sorry. I was miles away.'

'Natalie's definitely not your average woman,' Ruth informed Fran with a grin. 'She actually glazes over at the mention of shoes.'

'Ah, but she understands chocolate,' Fran said. 'She's one of us.'

Natalie didn't mind the teasing. At least it got them off the subject of Kit.

But as if they'd read her mind, Fran asked, 'He's lovely, though—don't you think?'

Uh-oh. This was going in a direction she really, really didn't want to go in. Especially as she'd already learned that Fran and Ruth didn't take no for an answer. They kept asking. If she said she didn't think Kit was lovely, they'd want to know why. And she'd end up admitting that she used to be married to him. And why they'd split up. And Natalie really didn't want her past dragged up and discussed on the hospital grapevine. 'Handsome is as handsome does,' she said with a shrug.

* * *

Kit had been about to walk into the staffroom and grab a coffee when he heard the subject of the conversation.

The nurses on the ward thought he was gay?

Some joke. He'd never been remotely attracted to another man, and he still appreciated pretty women. He just didn't do relationships any more. There was no point, not since he'd lost the love of his life.

The woman who'd just walked back into his life—but had made it very clear that she didn't want to resume where they'd left off. They were barely even friends now. Such a waste, when he remembered what they'd once been to each other.

Handsome is as handsome does.

The scorn that had gone into that remark. OK, so Natalie had good reason to feel that way. He'd let her down in the worst possible way, at the worst possible time. And he hadn't tried hard enough to save the remnants of their marriage, because he'd been focusing on keeping himself together. Burying himself in work, keeping himself so busy that he hadn't had time to hurt. Hadn't gone under. And he hadn't paid enough attention to what was happening to her.

But, oh, that comment rankled. Natalie thought he was shallow?

Maybe, just maybe, he *should* be shallow. Accept all the offers thrown at him. Have wild sex with a different woman every night.

Except that wasn't who he was. Wasn't what he wanted.

As for what he did want… He was just beginning to work out what that was. And it simply wasn't an option.

He turned on his heel and headed back towards his office.

CHAPTER FOUR

ALL those years since the divorce, Natalie had managed not to think of Kit. Not to wish. But now, having to work with him and seeing him every day… It brought it all back. How much she'd loved him. How right it had felt to be in his arms. How her world had collapsed in on itself when she'd realised she'd lost him.

Ah, hell. She had to get over this—and she had to keep working here with him for the next six months, or it'd look as if she couldn't handle her first job as a doctor. As if she wasn't reliable. 'Personal reasons' wasn't a good enough reason to give up the post. It'd make future consultants chary of offering her a post on their ward in case she only lasted a couple of weeks there, too.

She'd worked too damned hard for this. She had to stick it out.

And she was determined to get Kit Rodgers out of her system. Once and for all.

So, for the next month, Natalie managed to keep herself under control. She worked hard, had an occasional evening out with her colleagues—once she'd made sure that Kit wasn't going to be there—and was really settling in.

Until the night of the ward's Hallowe'en fundraiser.

She'd tried to get out of it. 'I'll buy a ticket, sure, but I'll be on duty.'

'No, you're not,' Fran said. 'I've already checked. You're on an early that day. And even if you were on a late…' the look she threw Natalie said that she knew Natalie was perfectly capable of changing her duty if she thought it would get her out of the party '…you'd still catch the last three hours of it. So you're going. No arguments.'

'But—'

'No arguments,' Fran repeated, holding up a hand in protest. 'And you don't have to make your own costume, before you try using that as an excuse. You can hire one.'

Another of her arguments knocked down before she'd even voiced it, Natalie thought with an inward sigh.

'I'm not good at parties.' Not any more.

'You'll be fine at this one. You'll know virtually everyone there, and it's the fundraiser for our ward. You can't not be there.' Fran fished a leaflet out of her locker and gave it to Natalie. 'This is the supplier most people use for costumes. We've been running the night for a few years now, so they give us a percentage of their takings. You'll love it, Natalie. It's great fun, and it raises a hell of a lot of money for the ward. We've got a brilliant band. One of the surgeons fancied himself as a guitarist until he went to med school, one of the midwives sings, one of the Theatre nurses is on keyboards and somebody's brother is their drummer. They play everything, from the old classics through to chart hits. The food's great. And the raffle has to be seen to be believed. You can win a flight in a hot-air balloon, a day at a spa in that posh place that opened just up the road, a rally drive, a—'

'OK, OK. I'll buy raffle tickets,' Natalie said faintly. 'Lots of tickets.'

'Good. But you're still going to the party, even if I have to pick you up and drive you there myself,' Fran warned.

Natalie sank into an armchair. 'You know, when you make nursing director, all the doctors are going to be absolutely terrified of you. With good reason.'

Fran laughed. 'They'll be fine, as long as they buy a ticket to the ball and a pile of raffle tickets.'

Natalie lifted her hands in supplication. 'Have pity on me. I'm only a baby doctor.'

Fran's grin broadened. 'That's a truly terrible pun. For that, you have to buy an extra raffle ticket.'

'I'm not going to get out of this, am I?' Natalie asked plaintively.

'Nope.' Fran ruffled her hair. 'Stop fretting. It'll be good for you. It's a chance to dress up a bit and—well, if you didn't have such short hair, I'd say let your hair down.' She grinned.

'Yeah, yeah.'

But Natalie bought a ticket to the ball and hired a costume: a little black dress with a spaghetti-strap top and a ballerina-length skirt with a jagged hem, teamed with long black fingerless lace gloves. She added a black haematite choker and a chiffon wrap embroidered with spiderwebs, then, for the first time in years, she put on a pair of spike-heeled black shoes.

The kind of shoes she'd worn when she'd been married to—

No. She wasn't going to think about Kit tonight. He was probably going to be there, but there'd be plenty of people she knew at the fundraiser so she could avoid having to spend any time with him.

She hoped.

She didn't usually wear make-up on the ward but that

night she went for the dramatic look, with dark eye shadow and blood-red lips, and long false nails varnished black. She stared at herself in the mirror for a moment, her vision blurring with memories of past Hallowe'en parties when she'd gone as a vampire or a ghost bride. Student parties. And that last one—Kit's first one as a house officer, when she'd been heavily pregnant and Kit had fussed over her all evening, terrified that her waters would break in the middle of the dance floor and making her sit out every other dance in case her ankles started swelling…

Memories.

Memories she'd have to put behind her if she was to have a hope in hell of getting through the evening.

Her stomach was churning with nervousness by the time she got to the party. But as soon as she handed her ticket in to the person dressed as a mummy, she was greeted by a squeal—a voice she recognised behind the mask. Fran.

'You look fabulous, Natalie!' Fran said. 'And those shoes are to die for. Go get yourself a drink and have a good time. Debbie and Ruth are somewhere around—they're both in mummy costumes, too.'

Natalie headed for the bar, and resisted the temptation to buy herself a large glass of wine and down it in one to calm her nerves. She settled for a small glass of red wine and sipped it slowly. And then she didn't get the chance to be nervous any more when Ruth and Debbie swooped on her. 'You look fantastic. Put that drink down and come and have a dance,' Ruth said, dragging her out onto the dance floor.

Kit really wasn't in the mood for a party. He was tired and out of sorts. This time of year was never good for him; there were too many painful memories. Memories he was pretty sure he'd seen in Natalie's face, too. She'd looked strained recently. But he'd promised Fran he'd turn up to the fund-raiser. Had it been just an ordinary ward night out, he'd have begged off. Said he had a headache, or something. But the Hallowe'en party wasn't just a party. They were raising money for new equipment for the ward so, as a senior doctor, Kit needed to show his face. Giving a cheque—even a large one—just wouldn't be good enough.

He'd stay for half an hour, and then he'd make some excuse and leave early. It was a shame he'd only been on a late shift, not on nights.

He showered, changed into his hired costume and gelled his hair back. He thought about putting talc on his face to whiten his skin—as he'd done for Hallowe'en parties as a student, when he'd gone with Tally and had needed little persuasion to throw himself completely into the spirit of the occasion—but he just couldn't bring himself to make the effort. Not tonight.

With a sigh, he locked his front door behind him and made his way to the hall.

Natalie knew the second Kit walked in the door, as if there was still some kind of radar system between their bodies. Every nerve-end was screaming to her that he was here, he was here, he was *here*—but she willed herself not to turn round and look at him. She kept her back to where she just knew he was standing, and continued dancing with Ruth and Debbie.

So what if Kit was here? She'd known about it, prepared for it, could deal with it. *Would* deal with it. He wasn't likely to ask her to dance. And if he did, she'd claim she needed to go to the loo or something. And she'd stay there until she was sure he'd moved on to dance with someone else.

* * *

Kit recognised Tally instantly. It was just like the first time he'd met her, twelve years ago, when they'd been at a crowded student party. Everyone else in the room had just faded away for him. There had been only Tally. Then she'd been dressed casually in jeans and a T-shirt, with her glorious dark curls spilling over her shoulders.

Now…she looked fantastic. Not as she'd done that first time: less curvy—too thin, in his opinion, though he supposed it wasn't his business any more—and with her hair cut in a short, gamine style. But she was still as beautiful as she'd been at eighteen. Still drew his eye.

What clinched it for him was the dress. It was perfectly demure, with a neckline barely showing her cleavage and the skirt falling below her knees. But she was wearing high heels with it. Like most of the female staff at the hospital, she wore comfortable flat shoes at work—they spent so much time on their feet, it was only sensible. But Tally had always loved shoes. Sexy, do-me heels. Like the ones she was wearing right now. It made him want to hoist her over his shoulder, carry her out of the room and settle their differences in the most elemental way. Skin to skin.

His body reacted instantly to the thought, and he sucked in a breath. Oh, Lord. He still wanted her as much as he'd done before they'd first become lovers. He'd known within seconds of seeing her that she was the girl he was going to marry. Lust, love at first sight, whatever you wanted to call it: she'd been the one. Nobody else had ever matched up to her.

Why, why, why had he ever been so stupid as to let her go?

Natalie did her best to ignore Kit, dancing with the other staff on their ward and accepting every offer of a dance that came her way. But then, as she was swung round by her partner of the moment, she caught a glimpse of him.

He looked absolutely gorgeous in a white Victorian-style dress shirt, dark trousers, a brocaded waistcoat, a bow-tie and a sweeping black velvet cape. A vampire in the best Bram Stoker tradition, dark and handsome and dangerous. The kind that no woman could resist.

Kit was easily the best-looking man at the ball. Everyone else faded into the shadows in comparison, just like they had, the first time she'd met him. Back then she'd only been aware of his blue, blue eyes and that easy smile that had made her heart do an instant somersault. Tonight he wasn't smiling. He was nursing a drink at the bar and looking grim. But, oh, his mouth. It made her want to reach out and touch him. Take him and make him smile again.

Oh, this was bad. She couldn't possibly still feel that way about Kit. Not after all the bad stuff that had happened between them. They'd been divorced for years. The last few months of her marriage had been the most miserable of her life, and she'd trained herself not to think about him any more.

But there hadn't been anyone in her life since Kit. She'd had offers, but she'd turned them down. Apart from the fact that she hadn't wanted to risk getting hurt again, she'd never felt that instant spark, that magnetic pull, with any other man.

And, from what the hospital grapevine said, there hadn't been anyone in Kit's life either.

Mentally, she stamped on the hopes before they had a chance to grow. It hadn't worked last time and Natalie didn't repeat her mistakes. Ever. She'd just have to avoid him.

Though that was easier said than done, when Kit actually came over to her. Laid one hand on her shoulder. It was the lightest, lightest contact—but it was his bare fingertips against her bare skin, and it made desire shimmer down her spine. Memories of when they'd touched each other much more intimately.

'May I have this dance?'

No, was her head's reaction.

And it must have shown on her face, because he said softly, 'Natalie, if you say no, the hospital grapevine's going to work overtime and there will be all sorts of rumours as to why you've danced with everyone else except me. They'll think you're avoiding me.'

She was.

'And they'll start asking questions.'

Which she definitely didn't want. She didn't think he did either.

'We work together. We're expected to socialise a bit.' Then he gave her a half-smile. One that almost had her knees melting. Oh, this was so unfair. He shouldn't still be able to have this effect on her, not after all these years.

'Dance with me. Just once. To show there are no hard feelings.'

She took a deep breath. If he could be mature about it, so could she. And it was a fast, uptempo song. Meaning she wouldn't have to actually touch him. 'OK.'

And she nearly got away with it. Except the band switched seamlessly into playing a slow number—and, before she realised what was happening, she was in Kit's arms. Dancing with her head resting against his shoulder, the way she'd done so many times before.

Like their wedding day. He'd been wearing a brocade

waistcoat that night too. She'd been in a strapless boned dress, and his arms had been round her just like this. Their first dance had been to a Nick Drake ballad—a quirky choice, but a song they'd both loved—and there had been a smile on her face a mile wide. How happy she'd been. How happy they'd *both* been.

It was like coming home. Natalie was thinner than Kit remembered and he couldn't tangle his fingers in her gorgeous hair any more, and she wasn't even wearing the same perfume, but he remembered the softness of her skin. He remembered the feel of her in his arms, just like this. The way they'd danced on their wedding day, with her head resting against his shoulder in absolute trust that he'd never let her down, that he'd always be there for her.

Though he hadn't been.

He'd messed up, big time. And he'd never been able to get through the barriers she'd put up in defence. She'd shut him out and all that love had just drained away, like the sea at low tide.

Except, for him, it was still there. And now she was in his arms again, it was trickling back up. Threatening to flood his senses.

His head knew he should stop dancing with her, make some excuse and leave the party.

His heart wouldn't let him do it. He just needed to kiss her. Right here, right now. Just once. One tiny, tiny touch of his mouth against her skin. He dipped his head so that his mouth was resting against the curve of her neck.

Oh, bliss.

She still tasted as good as he remembered. He couldn't help tightening his arms round her waist, moving his mouth up the sensitive cord at the side of her neck. She shivered, but she didn't move away.

Kit was lost entirely. He closed his eyes, shutting out the rest of the world so it was only him and Tally. He brushed her earlobe with his lips, then her cheek— oh-h-h, and finally her mouth, so warm and sweet.

It was meant to be just one kiss. One tiny, gentle little kiss. But then her mouth opened underneath his, and he was really kissing her.

It was heaven, having Tally back in his arms, with her hands wound round his neck and her fingers in his hair and her mouth against his. His arms were wrapped so tightly around her that he could feel every movement she made.

He'd missed her so badly.

And now she was back. In his arms. Holding him. He splayed one hand against her back, let the other fall to the curve of her bottom. Lord, Lord, Lord, this was good. What he'd wanted to do ever since the moment he'd seen her again. Holding her close.

Kit had no idea that the song had changed, that the band had gone uptempo again, until someone bumped into them.

The music crashed into his senses and it was like being doused in cold water.

He pulled away from Natalie. He could see the shock in her eyes—no doubt it was mirrored in his. Oh, God. They'd just made one hell of a spectacle of themselves on the dance floor, kissing through God only knew how many dances, and the hospital grapevine was going to go absolutely crazy over this. The rumours had probably already started.

Natalie was shaking. Kit's first instinct was to drag her back into his arms, shield her from all the inquisitive glances with his body, but her barriers were back in place again. Her face was shuttered and she gave him a look that said, Don't come anywhere near me.

To hammer the point home, she took a step backwards. 'We shouldn't have done that.'

Yeah, he knew.

Except he couldn't help wishing they hadn't stopped.

What had they done?

Oh, God. She wasn't going to be able to face anyone in this room ever again.

She'd been kissing Kit. *Really* kissing him. In public. *Oh, God.*

And even though she desperately wanted to bury her face in his shoulder, feel his arms round her again, she couldn't do it. She couldn't go over the same old ground. Yes, she could lose her heart to him—but then he'd let her down again. He wouldn't be there when she needed him. And she couldn't bear it to happen a second time.

'We—we can't do this.' Her voice was shaking, but she forced herself to sound calm. 'If anyone asks, I was tipsy and so were you.'

'Tal—' he began, but she cut him short.

'Excuse me. I'm tired. I'm going home.'

A muscle flickered in his jaw. 'I'll see you home.'

'You honestly expect me to leave here with you?' Oh, no. No, no, no. She didn't trust him, and she trusted herself even less. If he saw her home, they'd end up in her bed. Because that spark was definitely still there between them. Within seconds of being in each other's arms again, they'd been kissing. In public.

In private, she knew that neither of them would be able to stop. That they'd be ripping each other's clothes off, desperate to touch each other's skin again. That they'd make love all night long, exploring and touching and tasting and remembering. Wiping out the bad and replacing the pain with good feelings.

It was so very, very tempting.

But it wouldn't last. Couldn't last. And she didn't want people talking about her, speculating about her love life. 'No way. I'll get a taxi. I'm not having everyone thinking we've spent the night together,' she said between clenched teeth. 'That kiss shouldn't have happened. And we're going to forget it did.'

Ah, who was she trying to kid? No way would she be able to forget it. Her whole body was yearning for him again. She'd missed him so badly. And how she wanted to feel his body curled around hers. How she wanted to go to sleep in his arms, feeling his heartbeat against her body and hearing his breathing go slow and deep and regular as he, too, drifted towards sleep. And then he'd wake her in the middle of the night by kissing his way down her spine, nuzzling her skin and making those tiny little murmurs of pleasure as he explored her body. They'd make love in the small hours and see the whole universe explode…

But it wasn't going to happen. She was going to let her head rule her heart on this one. She was going to be sensible.

'At least let me wait with you until your taxi arrives,' he said.

She shook her head. 'I'm going home, Kit. Alone. I don't want to be with you.' It was a lie, and no doubt he knew it, too. She wanted to be with him. Yearned to be with him. But she didn't want the pain that she knew would go with it.

'You're still not waiting on your own for a taxi,' he insisted.

She rolled her eyes. 'Stop being so overprotective. This is a hotel, Kit. I'm going to be in the foyer. I'll be perfectly safe.'

'You could be waiting for hours. It's Hallowe'en, Natalie. Parties everywhere. Taxis will be like gold dust. No, I'm taking you home.' The temperature of his voice dropped several degrees when he added, 'And, just in case you're thinking that, I'm not going to leap on you. You've already made it perfectly clear you're not interested. I've never forced myself on a woman and I'm not going to start now.'

Kit didn't even need to *ask* women, let alone anything else. They just fell at his feet, instantly captivated. Even when half the ward had been convinced he was gay, they'd found him incredibly sexy.

And tonight she'd just proved his sexuality. Kit Rodgers was absolutely, definitely not gay. Tomorrow's rumour mill was going to be unbearable. Especially if someone saw her getting into his car and assumed they'd gone off somewhere together to finish what they'd started on the dance floor. 'Kit, I...'

He rolled his eyes. 'For your information, I'm bloody tired and I'm not in the mood for a party. But I'll drop you home and show my face back here, just so nobody thinks I've had my wicked way with you.'

Put like that, it made her sound...childish. She squirmed. 'Kit, I...'

'Let's just get your coat and get out of here,' he said coolly.

'I haven't got one. Just this wrap.' Which was hardly sensible attire for a night at the end of October.

Especially, she thought as they left the hotel and stepped into the car park, as it was so frosty outside. She tried really hard not to shiver, but then her teeth started chattering.

Kit gave her a speaking look, removed his cape and slung it round her shoulders.

Still warm from his body heat. It was like having his

arms round her all over again. Oh, Lord. She couldn't cope with this.

'Don't,' he warned, before she could protest. 'You're cold.'

And he'd always had that gentlemanly streak. Good manners.

He opened the passenger door for her, but to her relief he didn't lean over to fasten her seat belt. Good. Because if he leaned over her, she might just be tempted to slide her hands into his hair and kiss him.

Ha. Anyone would think that small glass of red wine had gone to her head.

Then she remembered something. 'Didn't I see you nursing a drink at the bar?'

'Mineral water.'

Oh. Well, of course Kit would be responsible. He'd never drink—not even one glass—and drive. 'Sorry,' she muttered.

'No problem. Where do you live?'

She gave him her address.

'Right.'

He drove her there in silence. Didn't switch on the stereo either, she noticed—and Kit had always been such a music junkie. He'd either had a CD playing or had been humming some song or other under his breath.

He'd sung lullabies to Ethan, the sound of his pure, clear tenor voice bringing tears to her eyes.

She dragged in a breath and huddled deeper into her seat. Bad move, because she was still wearing his cape. Still had his bodily warmth surrounding her. And how much she wanted to feel his arms round her now.

He managed to find a parking space right outside her flat.

'I'll wait until you're in safely.'

His voice was cool, clipped. She didn't bother arguing.

She simply undid her seat belt, opened the passenger door and climbed out. She was about to close the door again when she remembered—she was still wearing his cape on top of her wrap. Quickly, she slid it from her shoulders, folded it neatly and left it on the seat. 'Thank you for the lift.'

'I'll head back to the fundraiser now. And I'll make sure everyone knows your honour is intact. I drove you home because you had a headache.'

Heartache, more like. 'Thank you.'

He waited until she'd opened her front door, stepped inside. Then he drove away. Left her alone. Just as she'd wanted him to. The dark, dangerous vampire leaving his prey.

Though in some ways it was already too late. Kit had stolen her heart all those years ago and had left it in splinters. She'd never be able to give it to anyone else.

She closed the front door behind her. Showered and washed her hair, as if she could wash all the memories and feelings away. But even the citrussy shower gel she favoured couldn't stop her remembering the scent of Kit's skin, warm and familiar, comforting and incredibly sexy, all at the same time.

Hell, hell, hell. She just had to remember they were different people now. Living different lives. Apart, not together.

And that was the way it was going to stay.

CHAPTER FIVE

To Natalie's relief, Kit was on a late shift the next morning rather than an early. She avoided the staffroom and kept her mind firmly on the ward round or doing paperwork, but Ruth and Fran caught up with her at lunchtime and marched her off to the canteen with them.

'Spill the beans,' said Fran. 'Now.'

'I don't know what you're talking about,' Natalie lied.

'That was quite some clinch you had with our registrar last night,' Ruth said with a grin.

Straight to the point. Well, she'd known she wouldn't get away with it.

'Two and a half dances' worth of clinch,' Fran added. 'Only one of them was a slow dance, too.'

Two and a half dances? Lord, had it been that many? It had felt like…seconds.

No, worse than that. It had felt like coming home.

'So we were completely on the wrong track about Kit, weren't we?' Ruth asked. 'He's not gay at all.'

'No,' Natalie muttered.

'And he took you home,' Fran said thoughtfully.

'Because I had a headache,' Natalie protested. Surely

he'd told them that. He *had* gone back to the party, hadn't he? 'I was going to get a taxi.'

'But he went all manly on you and insisted that he take you home.' Ruth looked at her. 'It's all right, don't panic. We know he didn't stay the night. And he wasn't gone long enough for you two to have…' She grinned. 'Well.'

Natalie's face flamed as she got the implication. No. Kit wasn't into quickies. Most of the time he'd preferred slow and easy. Taking his time. Enjoying every second of their love-making.

'He danced with every woman in the room when he came back, though I have to say nobody else got the sort of clinch out of him that you did,' Fran said. 'Or even a peck on the cheek, come to think of it.'

Natalie wasn't sure whether she was more relieved or horrified.

'And he helped clear up at the end,' Ruth added.

Which meant he'd stayed late. Despite the fact that he'd been tired. Because he'd been trying to make sure that everyone had seen him and nobody questioned her about vanishing with him the next day. Guilt throbbed through her. 'Oh.'

Fran raised an eyebrow. 'So *are* you seeing him, then?'

'No. Absolutely not.' That was the honest truth. She wasn't seeing Kit. And she wasn't planning to either.

But neither of them looked convinced.

Hardly surprising, seeing as she'd made such an exhibition of herself last night. Lost control. Forgotten the world, when she'd been back in Kit's arms. She needed an excuse, and she needed one fast. 'Look, I just had too much to drink last night.'

Fran and Ruth exchanged a glance that said they didn't believe her.

Again, hardly surprising. Even though Natalie didn't drink very much or very often, one glass of wine wasn't enough to make her throw herself at someone the way she'd thrown herself at Kit last night.

Had she thrown herself at him? Or had he thrown himself at her? Either way, they'd both gone up in flames at the first touch.

'You knew each other years ago, didn't you?' Ruth asked.

Natalie squirmed in her seat. 'Yes.'

'So is there something you're not telling us?'

More than something. But she didn't want to talk about the wreck of her marriage. 'Please, just leave it. I... It's something I'd really rather not discuss,' she said, rubbing her hand over her face and wishing she was a million miles away.

The strain must have shown in her eyes because they immediately changed the subject. And Fran bought her a frothy cup of hot chocolate and a blueberry muffin. 'An apology for pushing you,' she said with a rueful smile. 'Obviously you two were an item at some point and things went wrong. I'm sorry I embarrassed you or dredged up bad memories.'

Which only made Natalie feel worse: the two nurses meant well and she'd grown friendly with them in the weeks they'd worked together. 'It's not necessary. No offence taken.'

'Good, because I'd hate to make you feel bad.' Fran looked thoughtful. 'He's a nice guy, Natalie. He's lovely to work with. I can only assume he's the same outside work—and you're great, too. I can see the two of you would be good together.'

'Mmm.' Natalie shifted in her seat.

Fran sighed. 'And I'm putting my size fives in it again.

OK, I'll shut up. I won't ask what happened.' Even though she was clearly dying to know—just when had Natalie and Kit been an item, and why had they split up?

'Thanks.' Though it wasn't Fran and Ruth that Natalie was really worried about. It was the grapevine. And Kit's reaction. They were going to have to work together later today—and things were going to be really, really awkward.

Nobody actually said anything to Kit when he came on duty, but he was well aware of the speculative glances. Which meant that people had been talking. Oh, Lord. Natalie would really hate being the subject of grapevine gossip. And when he'd kissed her, he hadn't stopped to think about whether she was seeing anyone else. He'd completely blanked that thought from his mind, right from the start. So, for all he knew, he could've wrecked whatever relationship she was in right now. Caused problems between her and her new love—because no man would take kindly to the news that his partner had been giving someone else hot, wet kisses in the middle of a dance floor. To the point where she hadn't even noticed the song changing from a slow dance to something fast and upbeat.

Then again, Natalie wouldn't have kissed him like that if she were seeing another man. The Natalie Wilkins he knew had integrity. In spades. Which meant she had to be single.

Ah, hell. This was worse than being a teenager going through hormonal changes. He was in a flat spin—and all because his ex-wife had kissed him. His *ex*-wife. He needed to remember that. It was over between them.

Though he wished to hell it wasn't. That he could turn back the clock and change things—even if he hadn't been able to save Ethan, he could have done things differently.

Shared his loss with the one person who'd understood, instead of burying himself in work. Opened up to her. Let her open up to him. They should have helped each other through it, instead of letting it blow them apart.

He leaned his elbows on his desk and rested his forehead on his clasped hands. What a mess.

There was a rap on his open door and he looked up. 'Are you all right, Kit?' Debbie asked, sounding concerned.

'Fine, thanks,' he lied.

'Hmm,' was all Debbie said. Clearly she didn't believe him, but at least she didn't grill him. Just as well. He didn't want to talk about it.

'What can I do for you?' he asked, switching back into professional mode.

'Your clinic's starting in ten minutes. Do you want a coffee?'

'No, I'm all right. But thanks for the offer.' He smiled at her.

He got to hear little bits from the grapevine over the next couple of hours. Natalie wasn't seeing anyone—oh, and just why did he feel so pleased about that?—but everyone was speculating about the mystery man in her past. As the story went, there had been someone in her past who'd hurt her badly, and she'd buried herself in work ever since.

Ouch, thought Kit. That'd be me.

And it seemed she'd reacted to losing him in just the same way he'd reacted when they'd lost Ethan. Work, work and more work. Pushing herself harder and harder so she hadn't had a chance to feel the pain. Running from it.

The grapevine also had a lot to say about the man who'd let Natalie Wilkins get away. What an idiot he must have been, not to see what a lovely girl she was. Beautiful and clever—and nice with it. A real diamond.

Ha. He knew all that. And the grapevine was spot on. He was an idiot. He should have fought a lot harder for his marriage. Turned to his wife instead of his work to heal his broken heart. Pulled together with her, instead of letting the cracks between them grow wider and wider and wider until their marriage had crashed into the abyss.

Irreconcilable differences? Maybe. But they should both have tried a hell of a lot harder to sort them out.

Somehow he got through a clinic, forcing himself to concentrate on his patients instead of thinking about Natalie. He was fine when he was working. The problem was the time in between.

He was walking along the corridor, reading a set of notes, when he literally walked into her and dropped his file.

'Sorry!' He dropped to the floor and scrabbled for the bits of paper. Though it was a relief: it meant he had enough time to get himself under control again. So she wouldn't see the longing on his face.

'Are you all right?' he asked, when he'd got the file back together and stood up again.

'Uh-huh.'

She didn't sound all right. He wanted to pull her into his arms, hold her close, tell her everything was going to be fine—except when he reached out a hand to touch her, she flinched and pulled away.

Clearly she loathed him so much she didn't even want him near her. It felt like a knife twisting in his heart, but he forced himself not to react. Just dropped his hand. 'That's good,' he said briskly, as if nothing had happened. 'See you, then.'

Somehow he found the strength to walk away. Natalie was just a colleague who'd met him briefly in the corridor on the way to see a patient. And he'd do well to remember that in future.

Natalie added enough milk to her coffee so it would be cool enough to gulp down. Right now, she really needed a caffeine hit. When the staffroom door opened, she froze, ready to flee if it was Kit.

But it was Debbie, who took one look at her and frowned. 'Are you all right, love?'

'I'm fine.'

'You don't look it.'

'I'm fine,' Natalie repeated. If she said it enough, maybe she'd even start to believe it.

'If you need a friend to talk to—someone who won't repeat a word to anyone else—you know where I am,' Debbie said quietly.

Natalie gulped her coffee. 'Thanks, but…' She couldn't repeat the lie again. 'It's just this time of year,' she said. 'It's a bit difficult for me. Personal stuff. But I'd rather not talk about it, if you don't mind.'

'Is it to do with Kit?' Debbie asked, her voice gentle.

Oh, yes. Kit and their baby. But she couldn't handle anyone's pity. Been there, done that, cried way too many tears. 'Sorry, Debbie. I can't talk about it. Not even to you. Let's just say Kit and I used to be an item. And it was over a long time ago.'

The senior sister nodded. 'I guessed as much.'

Natalie wrapped her hands around her mug, willing herself not to drop it. 'Is everyone talking about it?' she whispered. 'Last night, I mean?' When she and Kit had been kissing each other stupid on the dance floor?

'It'll die down,' Debbie said with a reassuring smile. 'Just ignore it. Someone else will knock you off the gossip spot by the end of the day. You won't be the only pair who…well. These sort of things happen at a party.'

Natalie flushed. 'I just feel so stupid.'

'Want me to have a word with Lenox and see if we can get you two rostered on different shifts?' Debbie asked.

The tears almost spilled over, but Natalie blinked them back. 'Thanks, Debbie. It's kind of you to offer, really it is. But we're both adults and I can deal with this.'

'Hmm,' Debbie said. 'He looks as bad as you do today. Maybe you two need to talk.'

'Maybe.' But the time for talking had long since gone.

Kit and Natalie were both on the same shift the following day. Early. And they were rostered in the PAU again.

Kit looked like hell. There were dark smudges under his eyes, as if he hadn't slept properly. Join the club, Natalie thought. She wasn't getting a lot of sleep either. And probably for the same reason.

They really had to stop tearing each other apart. Learn to work together, for the ward's sake. And one of them was going to have to make the first move: it may as well be her.

'Want a coffee, Kit?' she asked.

He stared at her for a moment, as if not quite believing that she was using his name rather than a formal title. Then he smiled, and his whole face seemed to light up. 'Thanks. That'd be good. I didn't have time for breakfast this morning.'

'Me neither.' Not strictly true. She'd made some toast

but the first mouthful had choked her and she'd ended up crumbling it on her plate.

He pulled a chocolate bar out of his pocket and offered it to her. 'Want to share?'

Just like old times. Times when they hadn't had time for breakfast because they'd been almost late for lectures. And she'd met him for coffee between lectures—coffee and a bar of chocolate. Hardly a sensible diet. But they'd been so happy...

They couldn't go back. But maybe they could find a way forward. Find some kind of peace.

Their first case was a five-year-old boy with a fever and an abscess on the sole of his right foot.

'Harry was playing in the back garden,' his mum said. She sighed, shaking her head. 'He's such a monkey. I can never get him to wear shoes outside, even in winter. And I've given up hope of him ever wearing a T-shirt that isn't mud-coloured within ten minutes.'

Kit smiled. 'I was the same at his age.' He ruffled the little boy's hair. 'It's not as much fun playing unless you get really muddy, is it, Harry?'

The little boy managed a wan smile.

'So what happened?' Natalie asked.

'He came in, hopping on one foot—said he'd stood on something sharp. I could see the thorn in there, so I got the tweezers and I really thought I'd taken it all out. I put antiseptic on it and everything, and a plaster. But his foot's swollen and tender—and today blue stuff started coming out of it.'

'Can I have a look?' Natalie asked the little boy.

He nodded, and shifted in his seat. Clearly he was torn between being brave and wanting a cuddle with his mum.

Natalie smiled at him. 'If you sit on your mum's lap, Harry, it'll be easier for me to see it,' she said. 'Does it hurt a lot?'

'Yes,' he whispered.

'I'll try very, very hard not to make it feel bad.'

He looked slightly happier. Natalie gently took off his trainer and sock. Now for the crunch—removing the plaster was going to hurt.

'I need your help here, Harry,' she said. 'Do you know any magic words?'

'No.' His bottom lip wobbled.

Kit clearly guessed what she was planning, because he came to the rescue. 'I do. What we're going to do is say a magic word, really fast, and then Natalie can see your foot properly.' He smiled at the little boy. 'Abracadabra.'

'Abracadabra,' the little boy repeated.

'Faster,' Kit urged. 'And again. And again. And—'

The plaster was off. She glanced up at him, nodding her thanks, and returned her attention to the child's foot. Just as Harry's mother had said, it was swollen and tender, and the puncture site was oozing a bluish-green substance. It looked really nasty. 'You've been ever so brave, Harry,' she said. 'In fact, I think you definitely deserve one of my bravery stickers.' She'd copied Kit's habit of keeping a pack of stickers in her coat pocket. 'I just need to do a couple of things first. Do you think you can be brave for just a teeny bit longer?'

He nodded.

'When did it happen?' she asked Harry's mum.

'About a week ago.'

'You did exactly the right thing with the thorn,' Natalie said, 'but I'd say there were some bacteria on the thorn, something that went deeper into the tissues than your antiseptic did, and it took hold. There are a couple of likely candidates—*Staphylococcus* or *Streptococcus*—but I think it's more likely to be *Pseudomonas*. It's a bacterium you often find on decaying wood, and it produces this blue-green pigment called pyocyanin—that's what turned the pus coming from his foot blue.' She stroked Harry's hair. 'We'll get you sorted out and back to normal, honey. But what we have to do now is take a tiny, tiny sample of the gungy stuff so I can send it to the lab and get them to grow it for me, just to make sure I've got the right bacterium. Then I'm going to clean up all the gungy stuff and give you some special medicine that'll zap the bugs for you.'

'Will it hurt?' he asked, his voice wobbling slightly.

'I'll try very hard not to hurt you, sweetheart,' she said. 'But I tell you what. While I'm sorting your foot out, do you want to listen through my stethoscope and hear what your heart sounds like?'

'Can I do Mummy as well?'

'Sure you can.' She tipped her head on one side and looked at Kit. 'Want to do the honours and teach him how it works?'

Kit, obviously realising that she needed to distract the little boy, smiled back. 'Yep. And then you can tell all your friends at school everything you learned today,' he said to Harry.

While he was soothing their patient, Natalie quickly took a sample and labelled it for the lab, then put some local anaesthetic into the little boy's foot. Debridement—removing the infected tissue—was necessary to stop the infection spreading further, but it was messy and it could hurt, even with a local. She worked as quickly as she could, then applied a dressing. 'I'm going to keep him in for a while because we need to give him the antibiotics through a drip for the first couple of days, then we can switch to antibiotics in a liquid form so you can take him home. You'll need to give the medicine to him four times a day and make sure he finishes the course, even if his foot looks tons better, because otherwise the infection might come back.' Not finishing a course of antibiotics also meant that bacteria could develop resistant strains.

'We'll get you booked in upstairs and introduce you to the nurse who will be looking after him. You can stay with him for as long as you want,' Natalie said, 'and there's a parents' phone so you can give the number to anyone who needs to get in touch with you here.'

'But he's going to be all right?'

'He's going to be absolutely fine.' Natalie smiled at her. 'And now I believe someone around here deserves a big bravery award.' She handed the little boy a sticker, then took them up to the ward and introduced them to Fran.

On her return, Kit asked, 'What have you written him up for?'

'Broad-spectrum,' she said. 'Something that will cover staph and strep as well—but I'm pretty sure it's *Pseudomonas*.'

'Good call,' Kit said.

'Well, it was pretty much a textbook case. The colour of the pus—that bluey-green—was a give-away. Poor little mite.'

'You've got a nice way with patients,' Kit said. 'You re-assured the mum, told them exactly what you were going to do and threw in a bit of distraction for the bits of treat-ment that were going to hurt.'

'You did the distraction for me. Both times.'

He shrugged. 'Teamwork. It's what keeps a ward going.'

He didn't say any more, but she could see it in his eyes.
And we make a great team. Always did.

Yeah. But from now on it would be strictly professional.

CHAPTER SIX

THE morning of Ethan's birthday, Natalie dragged herself out of bed.

How could the sun possibly shine on such a day?

Everything felt like lead. It reminded her of the Emily Dickinson poem she'd studied for her A-levels about reactions after great pain. 'The hour of lead', Dickinson had called it. First—chill—then stupor—then the letting go…

Today Natalie was back in stupor mode. And she'd be there for the next six weeks. Remembering and wishing and keeping a lid on everything. Moving mechanically, getting through the days moment by moment.

She couldn't face breakfast. And there was only one place she wanted to be today. She'd already ordered a spray of white roses from the florist's a few doors down from her flat. Once she'd picked them up, she drove to Litchford-in-Arden. Left her car in the gravelled car park at the side of the church. Then, too numb to feel the coolness of the air, she walked through the churchyard to the memorial stone.

The churchyard still overlooked fields, the heart of England. Bleak right now, with dark ploughed fields and bare trees stretched against the winter sky, but in the summer the fields shimmered with yellow corn, and the air was filled with birdsong.

This was where part of her heart would always lie. Part of the broken shards that would never be whole again.

There was a tiny spot of lichen on the white stone, she noticed with a frown. She set the roses to one side and emptied her carrier bag of the cream cleaner, toothbrush and bottle of water she'd brought with her. Then she dropped to her knees and cleaned the stone meticulously until it gleamed. Ran her fingers over the black carved letters. The date that had splintered her universe.

Ethan Rodgers, aged six weeks. Sleeping with the angels.

Nine words that couldn't even begin to express the pain. The regrets for what might have been. She'd never had the chance to see her little boy growing up. She'd seen his first smile, yes, but no first tooth, no tiny white crescent peering through his gums. She hadn't heard his first 'Mum-mum' or 'Dada', or seen his look of wonder when he'd first realised he could crawl, actually move under his own steam. No wobbly first steps. No splashing in the bath. No mum and toddler swimming class or baby group. No songs, no first day at school, no first nativity play as a shepherd in a dressing-gown with a teatowel on his head.

All the weight of the things they hadn't had time to do seemed to crash down on her. How could emptiness weigh so much?

'My baby,' she whispered. 'Happy birthday.'

It was a day when she should have made him a cake with six candles on it. A day when she should have been planning a party—maybe at one of the play centres where he and his friends could have jumped all over bouncy castles and burnt off their energy before the birthday tea, or maybe she'd have hired a magician to bring forth 'oohs' and 'ahs' with his magic tricks, and delighted laughter as he'd launched into the comedy routine that usually ended with a parent being teased silly.

And all she could do for her little boy now was bring him flowers. Flowers he wouldn't even see.

Shuddering with the effort of holding back the tears, she filled the little push-in vase with water, then arranged the white roses in it.

'Sleep tight, my angel,' she choked, and stood up again.

That was when she saw Kit.

He was leaning against the wall of the churchyard, carrying flowers, just watching her.

Their gazes locked. Blue on blue.

Well, he had as much right as she did to be here. She nodded once, and he walked over to join her at the grave.

'Sorry. I didn't mean to get in your way. I thought you might have gone by now.'

She lifted one shoulder in a half-hearted shrug. 'I've got no sense of time today.'

'Me neither.' He paused. 'Though I suppose when I was in London I always knew you'd have been here first thing, so when I got here in the afternoon we wouldn't have to face each other.'

'You drove here from London?' It was a good couple of hours' drive, even with the motorways.

His face tightened. 'Do you really think I wouldn't care enough to visit my son's grave on his birthday?'

She wrapped her arms round herself defensively. 'Sorry. I didn't mean it like it sounded. Of course you'd want to be here.'

'Oh, hell, Tally. Our baby.' He laid the flowers down and dragged her into his arms.

He was shaking, too. Shaking as much as she was.

Hurting as much as she was.

She slid her arms around his waist and held him tightly. Leaned against him, as he was leaning against her. And he was holding her the way she'd so wanted him to hold her all those years ago. Letting her know she wasn't on her own in this misery, that although things would never be completely all right again, they'd get through it. Together.

When she lifted her head, she saw that his sweater was wet. Wet with her silent tears.

'Sorry,' she whispered.

''S all right.'

One glance told her that he was in just the same state as she was. His eyelashes were damp and his eyes were suspiciously red.

He held her for a moment longer, then let his hands drop.

She loosened her hold on him, too, and backed away. 'I'll let you have some time alone with him.'

'Thank you.' His voice sounded cracked. Just as she turned to go, he whispered, 'Tally?'

She turned back. 'Yes?'

'Don't go.'

He wanted her to stay?

'I think…maybe it's time we talked. Wait for me?'

She nodded. And she noticed that, unlike her, he laid his flowers on the patch of grass in front of the gravestone. Maybe because he felt he didn't have the right to use the little vase where she'd put her flowers?

She knelt down beside him. 'Kit. There's room…if you want to.' She indicated the little vase.

He smiled wryly. 'I don't want to spoil your arrangement. I'm rubbish with flowers.'

'Do you want me to…?'

He nodded and handed her the stems of the yellow roses, one by one. He checked them first to make sure there were no thorns to hurt her, she noticed.

Yellow and white roses. Mingled together. Hers and his. For once, their son had united parents. United in their loss. Their longing. Actually visiting his grave at the same time—something they'd never managed to do before.

Her hands were shaking as she arranged the flowers in the vase. When she'd finished, Kit took her hand and raised it to his lips. 'Thank you,' he said softly.

And she knew he didn't mean just thank you for arranging the flowers. He meant thank you for sharing the moment. For not pushing him away from their baby's grave.

''S all right,' she said, echoing his earlier words.

He didn't let her hand go, she noticed. As he stood up, he drew her up with him. 'Let's go for a coffee somewhere. Not in Litchford-in-Arden, though.'

She knew what he meant. If they stayed here, the chances were they'd come across someone who'd known them when they'd lived there. Someone who'd maybe come to Ethan's funeral, almost six years before. Someone who'd remember and offer condolences neither of them wanted to hear. Someone who'd ask questions neither of them wanted to answer.

'There's a little café in Ashington.' The next village. 'It opened last year.'

He nodded. 'Sounds good to me. Let's take my car.'

She frowned. 'Why?'

'Unless parking's improved greatly…'

She knew what he meant. Parking spaces in the village were like gold dust. They'd be lucky to find one, let alone two. She wrinkled her nose. 'It hasn't.'

'My car, then.'

It felt weird, sitting in the passenger seat next to Kit as he drove them away from the churchyard. Unlike the last time he'd driven her somewhere, at Hallowe'en, there was no tension, no urgent need to run from him. But it was still strange. They hadn't been together in a car like this for years.

It felt even weirder not to rummage among his CDs to find one she wanted to hear. Kit kept his stereo switched off anyway, and she was relieved. If the radio had played some song or other that had meant something to them, she knew she wouldn't have been able to handle it right then.

Kit didn't bother making conversation until they'd collected their coffees from the counter and were sitting at a quiet table in the corner of the café.

'Ethan would have been at school now,' he said softly. 'In year one. He'd be reading and writing, drawing pictures of rockets and fire engines, maybe learning to swim.'

'What do you think he'd be like?' It was something she'd pondered so often. But she'd never shared it with anyone else, not wanting to hurt her parents or her sisters by asking.

'Looks-wise?' Kit shrugged. 'Blue eyes, dark hair. Tall. Beautiful.' He paused. 'He had your smile.'

'And your chin.'

'Personality—I think he'd have been cheeky. Full of fun. Interested in anything and everything.' His eyes darkened. 'Like you.'

'A charmer. Like you.'

He smiled wryly. 'Surface? No, our boy would've been

deep. You wouldn't have let him wrap you round his finger with a smile.'

Ha. Kit had been able to do that. Once.

'You'd have taught him right from wrong, good from bad. Encouraged him to explore. You'd have been a brilliant mum,' he added, his voice cracking.

Tears welled up in her eyes, and she scrubbed them away with the back of her hand.

Kit reached out to hold her other hand. 'Tally. I'm so glad…so glad I can talk about him.' His voice was rough with emotion. 'On his birthday. I…couldn't talk about him to anyone else.'

Not his parents, his brothers? Then again, the Rodgers family hadn't exactly approved of Ethan in the first place. He'd been unplanned. Bad timing: just when Kit had been starting his houseman year and had had enough pressure at work, without the added worry of having a newborn.

She and Kit hadn't made a baby on *purpose*.

But a termination had been completely out of the question. Neither of them had even considered it. Ethan might have been unplanned, but he'd been wanted. So very, very wanted. By both of them, and to hell with what Kit's family had planned for him.

But surely Kit had been able to talk to friends? To his— oh, God, the idea made her ache, but she had to face it— to his new partner? She knew he was single now, but had there been someone else? Had he tried to forget her, forget their baby, in another woman's arms?

She needed to know. 'I thought you'd be married again by now.'

He shook his head. 'There's been no one special.' There was a long, long pause. 'You?'

She shook her head. She hadn't been able to face the pain again. The pain of loving someone…and knowing that she could lose them. Just like she'd lost Ethan and Kit.

'I remember the day you told me you were pregnant. It was March. A day like today, when the sun was shining and the sky was blue and it was freezing cold, and you handed me that little package. It wasn't anywhere near my birthday so I didn't have a clue what it was. And I'd just come off a really, really heavy night shift. All I wanted to do was collapse into bed and sleep.' His smile was bleak. 'And then I saw they were babies' shoes. Little white satin pram shoes.'

'Expensive shoes.'

He lifted one shoulder. 'Since when did *you* ever buy cheap shoes?'

Just when she thought he was sniping, he added softly, 'And they were worth every single penny. I can't think of a better way to find out I was going to be a dad than unwrapping my baby's first shoes.'

Shoes they'd buried him in, later that same year. And the shawl her great-great-aunt had crocheted for him. In the tiny white coffin that had somehow seemed too small to contain their child.

Natalie didn't drag her hand away from Kit's. At that moment it felt right, holding his hand. A connection between them while they shared their memories.

'I remember the first time I felt him kick,' Kit said softly. 'My hand was just resting across you, and suddenly there was this wallop—as if he was saying hello, telling me he was awake, and would I mind moving my arm, please, because I was too heavy. And he used to get hiccups and wake you up at three in the morning with baby gymnastics. He had hiccups at the twenty-week scan, too. We could actually see it on the screen.'

Kit remembered that?

Again, Natalie felt tears film her eyes.

'And the day before he was born, you wanted to go to the beach. We lived smack in the middle of England, miles and miles away from a beach—and it was November, freezing cold, really not beach weather—but you really, really wanted to paddle in the sea.'

The strongest urge she'd ever had, and about the only time she'd ever regretted moving to the heart of England. 'And you looked on the map to find the nearest proper beach. You drove me all the way down the M5 to Weston-Super-Mare so I could walk on the sand and paddle in the sea,' Natalie recalled. It had taken them hours to get there.

'And you couldn't reach your feet over the bump to wipe off the sand when you'd finished paddling. I had to do it for you. And I was terrified you were going to go into labour before I could get you home again and I'd have to deliver our baby myself in the car.'

'My labour didn't start until three o'clock in the morning,' Natalie said. 'And somehow you managed to rub my back and sleep at the same time. Cat-napping. Junior doctor habit.' One she was learning, too.

'Yeah.' He smiled. 'I'd read all the textbooks. I worked out it'd probably be twelve hours before he arrived, so I didn't have to rush you in.'

'Except it took eighteen. And you fiddled with the remote control on the TENS machine and gave me full blast at the wrong time.' She smiled wryly. 'Typical male.'

'I had the bruises for weeks, you were gripping my hand so hard every time you had a contraction.'

Just like he was gripping her hand now.

'I remember the first time I held him,' Kit said softly. 'He was so beautiful. I couldn't believe he was really ours, that he was finally there. That we'd made something so very special.'

'And you slept in a chair that night by our bed.'

'I didn't want to leave you,' Kit said simply. 'I couldn't. My wife, my baby.' His breath hitched. 'My family.'

And they'd had so little time together. So very little time. Six short weeks, and ten days of them had been spent in hospital at Ethan's bedside.

But today they should remember the good bits. 'I remember his first smile,' Natalie said. 'You said it was just wind.'

'And then he did it again and I had to admit it was a real smile all right—of course he'd smile at his mum.' Kit's face softened. 'Remember the way he used to hold our fingers? You on one side, me on the other, just watching him as he lay between us in the middle of our bed. Fast asleep and holding onto both of us. Wearing that little white sleepsuit with the ducklings on it your youngest sister bought for him.'

'Yeah.' Moments when she'd thought her heart would burst with happiness.

'It's not fair,' Kit said, a muscle working in his jaw. 'It's not fair that we didn't get our chance. All the things we never got to do with him. I never gave him piggybacks or took him to feed the ducks or kick a ball around the park. I never taught him to ride a bike or swim or make sandcastles or skip stones in a lake—all the things a dad wants to do with his child.'

'Yeah, it's the might-have-beens that hurt the most.' She'd never had the chance to make him a birthday cake or read him stories or do finger-painting or play-dough with him.

And there was something else that had hurt her deeply. 'You were nearly late for his funeral.'

Kit exhaled sharply. 'I had an emergency at work. I couldn't just leave my patient on the operating table.'

It was good, as excuses went—but not good enough. 'You were a house officer, Kit. A junior doctor, not the lead surgeon. They could've found someone to take your place that morning, of all mornings.'

He didn't try to argue, she noticed. Clearly he knew she was right.

'I got stopped for speeding on the way to the church,' Kit said. 'But the policeman let me off when I explained where I was going and why.'

Maybe, but there was something he'd never explained to her. 'Why did you even go to work on that day? Why weren't you with me?' When she'd needed him so badly, when she'd needed the comfort of his arms round her, the day they'd laid their baby to rest? The day she'd had to walk behind the coffin on her own?

'Because I couldn't handle it,' he said softly. 'I couldn't handle the fact that Ethan was gone. That our beautiful baby had died. The only thing that made any sense to me was work, somewhere I was needed.'

'*I* needed you,' she burst out.

'I know.' He refused to let her hand go. 'I couldn't make things right for you, Tally. I couldn't save Ethan. I couldn't bring him back. But I could make things right at work. I could make a difference *there*.' His eyes held hers. 'I'm sorry I let you down. If I had the time over again, it'd be different.' He sighed and shook his head. 'Tally, we were both twenty-four years old. Hardly more than children ourselves. I was too young, too immature to deal with it properly.'

He had a point. And, deep down, she'd realised that at the time. But it had still hurt like hell. Kit had let her down. He had never been there. She'd been short-tempered, forever finding fault with whatever he'd done on the rare occasions he had been there. So he'd backed away even more, and the vicious circle had gone on and on and on. Pulling tighter and tighter, until finally the life had been squeezed out of their marriage.

'I hurt too much to see what was happening to you,' he said softly. 'I'm sorry. I was wrong.'

Not only him. 'Your oldest brother didn't even come to the funeral.'

Kit exhaled sharply. 'You know why. Melanie was six months pregnant. It would have been like rubbing our faces in it—and even if Julian had come on his own, without Mel, we'd still have been thinking about it. About the fact they were going to have a baby in three months' time, and we were burying ours.'

'And your parents blamed me.' For having Ethan in the first place—and then for him dying. Natalie had overheard that whispered conversation. And she'd never forgotten it. Or forgiven it.

Kit's face registered shock. 'But— No, Tally, that's crazy. He had a virus—Coxsackie B—and there were complications. Cardiomyopathy. He died of heart failure. It wasn't your fault.'

Maybe. But there'd always been that nagging doubt in the back of her mind. Supposing she'd done things differently? 'If I hadn't taken him out somewhere, he might not have picked up the virus.'

'Tally, it really wasn't your fault.' He squeezed her fingers. 'You know as well as I do that viruses are everywhere in winter. Coughs, colds, RSV, Coxsackie B…it's the time of year. You can't move a step without coming in contact with some microbial thing or other. And if you'd stayed stuck indoors with Ethan, maybe a visitor would have brought the virus with them—maybe it was something he *did* get at home. It could have been anyone who called at the door. The postman, the newspaper delivery boy—anyone. It really wasn't your fault. You know Coxsackie B can survive for days outside, even in freezing weather. Maybe *I* was the one who brought it home—maybe I'd come into contact with it at the hospital.' He stared at her. 'Please, tell me you haven't spent the past few years blaming yourself.'

'I… No.' She sagged against the back of her chair. 'Not really.'

'Good. Because it wasn't your fault. It wasn't anyone's fault.'

'That's not what your mother thought. I heard her talking at the wake.'

Kit shook his head, clearly not understanding. 'Why didn't you say something to me? I would've dealt with it. Put her straight.'

'Because you were never there,' she said simply. 'You just left me to deal with everything.'

'Maybe this was a mistake. Trying to talk.' He dragged in a breath. 'This isn't going to help either of us—going over old ground, old hurts. We can't change the past. I would've given my life to be able to save our son, Tally, but I couldn't. If anything, I failed him far more than you did. I was the qualified medic.'

'You weren't a paediatric specialist. Or a cardiologist. And even if you had been, it wouldn't have changed what happened. As you said, nobody could have saved him.' She wrested her hand free. 'Kit. We have to move on. Forget the past. Let's just leave things here.'

'So where does that leave us?'

'We're colleagues. At least until my six months is up.' She took a deep breath. 'And that's it. Kit, I need to go now.'

She hadn't touched her coffee, Kit noticed. Just as he hadn't touched his. He didn't have the stomach for it.

And those moments in the churchyard, where they'd held each other by Ethan's grave, that was past, too. A passing weakness in her eyes. It wasn't the beginning of maybe finding some common ground. It was closure.

The end.

And there was absolutely nothing he could do about it.

'I'll take you back,' he said quietly, and pushed his chair back. In silence, they left the café. Kit drove her back to Litchford-in-Arden. Watched her leave. Then walked back into the churchyard and sat by Ethan's stone.

'I wish I could turn the clock back,' he whispered, running the tip of his finger along the tightly furled petals of the rosebuds. 'I wish I could change it all. Bring you back. Not let you have that bloody virus in the first place. And then everything would be how it should have been.'

But he couldn't change a thing. And nothing he could do would fill the hollowness inside him.

CHAPTER SEVEN

THE problem was, Kit thought as he scraped his barely touched meal into the bin that evening, he still loved Tally. He hadn't contested her request for divorce because he'd been too numb at the time. He hadn't allowed himself to feel, in case he fell apart completely. And it had stayed that way ever since.

Until their lives had collided again.

The moment he'd seen her in the staffroom, he'd known. The moment he'd held her at the fundraiser, he'd been absolutely sure. She was his one and only.

And today, when they'd held each other, had been the first time he'd really cried since the day Ethan had died. Every birthday, every anniversary, Kit had brought flowers to Litchford-in-Arden. And he'd stood by his baby's grave, dry-eyed, wishing the wreckage of his life would somehow fix itself the way he fixed patients.

Right now, the wreckage seemed to be sliding further towards an abyss.

Natalie's words echoed in his head. *We have to move on. Forget the past. Let's just leave things here.*

In her view, they were just colleagues. *And that's it.*

It wasn't enough. Never would be enough.

But right now he didn't even know where to start trying to change things.

Natalie huddled in her chair, her knees drawn up to her chin and her arms wrapped around her legs. It was the first time she and Kit had talked—really talked—since Ethan had died. If only he'd told her how he had been feeling back then. If only he'd shared, let her in instead of shutting her out. But he hadn't, and she'd felt more and more alone. As if she had been the only one in their marriage.

In the end, she hadn't been able to stand it. She'd packed, left him a note, telling him that it was over and she wanted a divorce, and all communications from then on had been through a solicitor. Sighing, she remembered how her parents had tried to tell her that he was grieving in his own way, to give him a chance, but she'd refused to listen. All she'd seen had been that the love of her life hadn't been there when she'd needed him. He'd turned away. Thrown himself into his job. Shut her out.

For better, for worse…in sickness and in health.

Vows she'd meant when she'd taken them. Really, really meant.

Till death us do part.

She'd thought it would be her death, or his. Not their baby's.

Maybe they'd just been too young when they'd got married. Twenty-one. Both still students—Kit an under-graduate, Natalie studying for her post-graduate certificate in education. They had no money, lived in a rented cottage because they couldn't afford to buy anywhere, and their honeymoon was three days in a little bed-and-breakfast in a Cornish fishing village, because it was all Kit's bank account could stretch to and he insisted on sticking with the tradition that the bridegroom paid for the honeymoon.

But they were happy. So very happy. They laughed and loved and were just *together*. It didn't matter if they had to live on beans on toast by the end of the month, or that they didn't go out to flash restaurants. All they needed was each other.

Ethan's death changed all that. They weren't even able to share the good memories. They simply stopped talking. And when she left Kit, he didn't exactly try to get her back. Which proved to her that their marriage was finished. The day their divorce came through, she found out he'd moved to London.

It was all over.

So she'd started a new life. Talked her way onto a degree course in medicine, left her job as a history teacher and started the long haul to train as a paediatrician. The world of medicine was a pretty big one and she had no intention of working in London, so she'd never dreamed that her life would cross Kit's again.

Until the day he'd walked into the staffroom at St Joseph's.

She'd been lying to herself for years. Telling herself that she was over him. That she didn't date because she didn't want to end up in the same kind of mess, trapped in a marriage that no longer had love to hold it together. That she was focused on her career and she just wasn't interested in another relationship.

Ha. What she hadn't faced was *why* she wasn't interested in another relationship.

The truth was, she was still in love with Kit.

The way he'd kissed her at the fundraiser—it had been

like coming home. Like being fully alive again, seeing the world in colour instead of living from moment to moment in a monochromatic world. And she knew it had been the same for him, too. That he'd felt the same spark, the same need. Everyone else in the room had just melted away. They hadn't even heard the music change, they'd been so lost in each other.

But they couldn't go back. They couldn't change the past. And although it would be, oh, so easy to call him, go back to him, start their relationship all over again, she knew it would be a mistake. Because there would come a time when she'd need him—and he would let her down. Just like he had last time. People didn't change, not deep down. She couldn't afford to lean on him again—if she needed his support, she knew it simply wouldn't be there.

So they had to move on. Be professional about the fact they had to work together. In a few months, when her rotation in the paediatric department was over, she'd move to the emergency department for six months. She wouldn't see him again, except maybe if she referred a case to Paediatrics. And then, once her house officer year was over, she could change hospitals. Find another job on another children's ward, in another city, a long, long way from Kit Rodgers. Maybe move back to Bristol, where she'd done her training.

For now they were colleagues. Just colleagues. And that was how it was going to stay.

Over the next couple of weeks, Kit and Natalie were wary of each other at work. They were civil to each other on the occasions when they had to be in the same place at the same time, but both scanned the staffroom before they went in, and if Kit was there Tally would make some excuse about forgetting some paperwork, or if Tally was there Kit would invent a patient who needed to see him.

It was fine, as long as they didn't have to be too close to each other.

Kit wondered if Debbie had said something to Lenox, because he and Tally were rostered apart for a while. Or maybe she hadn't, because then they ended up working in the PAU together.

Kit flinched when he saw their first patient. A small girl, around two years old, carried in her father's arms. The mum was there, too—pregnant. About six months, he'd say, from the size of the bump. Her partner was making sure she was comfortable on the chair, clearly taking as much of the worry from her as he could.

Exactly what Kit had done when Tally had been pregnant with Ethan. Fussed over her, made sure she had everything she'd needed.

Exactly what he *should* have done when Ethan had died, instead of shutting the world and the pain out.

He shook himself. No. He had to concentrate on his job. Not the mess that was his personal life.

The little girl had definite stridor, harsh abnormal breathing that was caused by a narrowing or obstruction of the larynx or trachea. This would be a good case for Natalie—she'd need to work out if the stridor was being caused by croup, a foreign body, epiglottitis, a low level of calcium in the blood or one of the rarer causes.

'You lead,' he said to Natalie.

Natalie introduced Kit and herself to the Leonards, and discovered that little Gail was two years old.

'How long as she been like this?' she asked.

'Since yesterday. She's got this barking cough, and it was worse last night,' Mrs Leonard said.

'I know her breathing sounds scary, but we can do something to help,' Natalie reassured her. 'Small children have narrower airways, so they find it harder to breathe when they have a cough or cold. And coughs are usually worse at night when you've been lying down for a few hours. May I examine her?'

The Leonards nodded.

'And may I ask you something first? You said she's been like this since yesterday.'

'Except it's got worse overnight,' Mr Leonard said.

'Sometimes this kind of breathing's caused by inhaling something—a peanut or a bead, something small that blocks the airways. Is there any chance Gail could have inhaled something?' Natalie asked.

'No. We never have peanuts around the house, and she's always with me,' Mrs Leonard said. 'I'd have noticed if she'd put something in her mouth or up her nose or what have you.'

'That's fine. I just needed to rule it out before I examine her,' Natalie reassured her.

Kit watched her carefully. If she moved to examine the child's throat before ruling out the possibility of epiglottitis, he'd stop her. Epiglottitis, a bacterial infection that caused swelling of the epiglottis—the flap of cartilage at the back of the tongue that closed off the trachea and larynx when you swallowed—could become a medical emergency within seconds, because trying to examine the throat could cause a complete obstruction of the airway. It was something you could only do properly when the child had been intubated, and that needed an anaesthetist.

'Has Gail been immunised against Hib?' Natalie asked.

The *Haemophilius influenzae* bacterium was the cause of epiglottitis. The vaccination programme meant that fewer cases were seen nowadays, but if Gail hadn't been immunised, there was a chance that this was epiglottitis.

'All her vaccinations are up to date,' Mr Leonard confirmed, stroking his little girl's hair.

'Has she had a cough or cold over the last few days?' Natalie asked.

'Yes, a bit,' Mrs Leonard said.

'Have you noticed if she has any problems swallowing?' Natalie asked.

Kit relaxed. She was asking all the right questions, and little Gail wasn't drooling, so the chances were she wasn't having that much of a problem swallowing. It was unlikely to be a case of foreign body inhalation or epiglottitis, then.

'None,' Mr Leonard said. 'She's been a bit off her food, but we've got her to drink a bit.'

'I'll just check her temperature and listen to her chest,' Natalie said. She examined the little girl, and noted the measurements down on the file. 'She doesn't have a fever, and I can't hear any wheezing, so it's not a lower respiratory tract problem. I'm just going to check her throat, but I think she's got croup, which is very common in children of her age group at this time of year. Though she's finding it very hard to breathe and getting a bit tired, so I'm going to admit her for treatment.'

Kit glanced over her shoulder; she'd written, 'Rib recession—query croup—admit.'

'What I wanted to check is that she didn't have a condition called epiglottitis, which has very similar symptoms to croup. But her temperature's fine, she doesn't have problems swallowing and her breathing's very harsh, so we can rule that out,' Natalie continued. 'Croup is caused by a viral infection in her upper airway—most likely the parainfluenza virus.'

This time, she actually glanced at Kit; he knew what she was thinking. There were other viral causes—respiratory syncitial virus, influenza virus type A, rhinovirus…and Coxsackie virus.

The virus they both found so hard to handle.

'It's basically affected her throat,' Natalie explained. 'Do you have any other children?'

'Only Gail. And this little one.' Mrs Leonard placed a protective hand on her bump. 'Croup couldn't affect my baby, could it?'

'It's unlikely, but you might be a bit uncomfortable if you catch the same virus. The virus is transferred through airborne droplets, such as coughing and sneezing, and it's passed from one person to another by touch. It tends to go from your hands to the mucous membranes of your eyes and nose, so make sure you wash your hands a lot. You may also find that Gail gets croup the next time she has a cold,' Natalie warned. 'It may keep recurring, but the good news is that the symptoms aren't so severe once children get to about five.'

'Are you going to give her antibiotics?' Mr Leonard asked.

Natalie shook her head. 'They won't make any difference because it's a viral infection, not bacterial—but as she's having difficulty breathing we'll keep her in for a while and give her some humidified oxygen to help her, as well as some drugs through a nebuliser to widen her airways and make it easier for her to breathe. Croup usually clears up in three or four days, though you'll find that the barking cough lasts a bit longer. I'll take you up to the ward and get her booked in, and you can stay with her as long as you like. Try to keep her as calm as possible—I know it's hard, when you're worried, but if Gail sees you're worried it will upset her more, she'll cough even more and she'll start panicking.'

The little girl was snuggled against her father's chest, and Kit felt his heart contract.

Oh, God. Would it ever stop hurting? Would he ever stop wishing?

'When you get Gail home,' Natalie said, 'you need to keep eye on her. If she has any more breathing difficulty or looks a bit blue round her mouth, nose or nails, you need to call your doctor immediately or bring her back here, because it means she's not getting enough oxygen and she'll need a bit of help.'

'What can we do to help the cough?' Mrs Leonard asked.

'Cough mixture's a waste of time,' Natalie advised. 'The best thing you can do is sit her up to help her breathing—prop her up against plenty of pillows at night. Steam inhalation helps, but you can't really sit a child over a hot bowl with a towel over her head—apart from it being too much of a risk for burns, little ones find it much too scary. The best thing you can do is to sit her in a steamy bathroom—run a shower on hot for a few minutes, or run a hot bath, and keep the door closed so the air's nice and moist.' She smiled at them. 'Obviously I don't need to tell you to keep an eye on her so she doesn't fall in the hot water and get burned.'

'What about food? Should we stick to soft foods?'

'For now, yes, because they'll be easier for her to manage. Keep her meals light, because anything heavy might make her be sick, and get her to drink lots of cool fluids. Now, let me take you up to the ward and introduce you to the nurse who'll be looking after Gail while she's here.'

When she returned, Kit took her to one side. 'You handled that well. You checked the main causes of stridor before you examined her throat.'

'She didn't look toxic, so I didn't think it was epiglottitis—but I wasn't going to take the risk.'

'Good. You'll make an excellent doctor, Tally.'

'Thank you.' Her voice was very cool.

Hell, hell, hell. She was shutting him out again.

And he couldn't get that comment about moving on out of his head. What did she mean by that? Finding someone else? Starting another family—with someone else?

He hoped not.

He didn't want anyone else. And he couldn't handle the idea of seeing her with someone else. Of course he wanted Natalie to be happy—but, please, not with someone else. He couldn't bear the thought of finding out that she was pregnant, and not being the one who had the right to go to antenatal classes with her, see the wonder of their baby at the ultrasound scan, feel the baby kicking in her womb, or share those first precious seconds when a new life came into this world.

What he really wanted was to start again. Make a new life. With Tally.

But that meant persuading her to change her mind about him. And, right now, he didn't even know where to start.

CHAPTER EIGHT

NOVEMBER slid into December, the dark days of the year. The days Natalie always found hardest. The hospital was gearing up for Christmas—the tree in the reception area was decked with tinsel and baubles and coloured lights; there were cards from colleagues and past patients on the notice-board; the pictures of Santas and snowmen drawn by the older children were pinned up on the boards by their beds; and there were mince pies and chocolates and Christmas biscuits in the staff kitchen—but Natalie really couldn't get into the spirit of things.

She'd joined in the ward's 'Secret Santa' and, to her relief, she'd drawn Ruth's name out of the hat—if she'd picked Kit's, it would have been too much. Fran had also talked her into going for a Christmas drink with some of the staff before going to the hospital social club revue. But that was as much as Natalie could manage. That, and a forced smile as people wished her a merry Christmas.

Christmas hadn't been merry for a long, long time.

Probably never would be again.

And as the days dragged on towards the day of the year

she really hated, she grew quieter and quieter. She wanted to be on her own. Just quiet and thinking, and wishing things were different.

Kit knew Natalie had booked the day off. It stood to reason: today was a day when she wouldn't want to be around anyone. But she'd been so withdrawn lately, her face pale and pinched. And he was worried about her.

He rapped on Lenox's door and glanced through the window. At the consultant's nod, he walked in and closed the door behind him. 'Hi. Can I ask a huge favour, please?'

Lenox lifted an eyebrow. 'You want to swap your Christmas duty?'

Kit smiled. 'No, no, that's fine. I don't mind working at Christmas.' It was better than sitting on his own in a rented flat. And much, much better than heading south and spending the day with his family, following old traditions yet feeling out of place. Kit was the only one of his siblings who wasn't married with children—even though he'd actually been the first of the four to get married and the first to have a baby. Catching the occasional glances from his brothers, the looks that said, there but for the grace of God—it hurt like hell. The way his sisters-in-law tried to share their children with him, make him feel part of the family, encouraged the kids to make a fuss of their special uncle... Oh, he hated it.

He made the effort, always played nice, made a point of playing games with them and making sure he could talk to them about whatever the in thing was. But inside his heart always ached. Because it wasn't the same as doing it with his own child. And seeing his nephews and nieces was too much of a reminder of what he'd lost. What he hadn't had the chance to do. Like little ghosts of what Ethan might have been like at that age.

So Kit would much rather spend his time with the children on the ward instead. Helping them to get better. Doing something positive instead of inwardly brooding, hating the fact that his son wasn't there to open his stocking on Christmas morning. Losing himself in work instead of counting the seconds until he could escape for a walk on his own and not have to fake a seasonal jollity he simply didn't feel.

'What can I do for you, then?' Lenox asked.

Now for the tough one. 'I need Natalie's home phone number.'

Lenox shook his head. 'Sorry. I can't give out confidential staff information.'

Well, Kit had expected that. So now he had no choice but to explain. He took a deep breath. 'There's a good reason. I'm worried about her.'

'She's been a bit quiet lately,' Lenox agreed. 'I was going to have a chat with her, check she was happy on the ward or if she was worried about her work.'

'It isn't the job. It's the time of year.' Kit raked a hand through his hair. 'Look, can I tell you something in confidence? Something I don't want going any further?'

'Of course.'

'I should've told you this when I first came here.' Kit stared at the floor. 'Though I accepted the job before I knew Tally was going to be working here. I had no idea that she was even training to be a doctor, let alone newly qualified.' He sighed. 'I used to be married to her.'

'Ah.' There was a wealth of understanding in Lenox's

voice. 'So you need me to look at the rosters and keep you two apart?'

Kit wrinkled his nose. 'No, working together isn't a problem.' Well, it was—but it was *his* problem. He'd just have to deal with the fact that he was still in love with his ex-wife. 'Today's an anniversary.'

'Wedding?'

Bile rose in Kit's throat. 'I wish it was.' Framing these words were so hard. And he really couldn't bear to see the pity he knew he'd see in Lenox's face when he explained. But he had to do it. 'We had a baby. Ethan. He died six years ago today.' He dug his nails into his palms, reminding himself to keep this professional. To keep the emotion out of it. Just explain it in dry medical terms. 'He was six weeks old. Cardiomyopathy—a complication of Coxsackie B. We, um, split up not long after he died.' And that had been his fault. All because he'd shut Natalie out. Hadn't put her first when he should have done.

'I'm sorry,' Lenox said.

All the sorries in the world wouldn't bring Ethan back. And Kit really hated expressions of sympathy. Even when they were well meant, they rang a false note with him. He looked his consultant straight in the eye. Faced the pity. Right now, Natalie needed help. And Kit was going to put her first, above his own feelings. 'I could ring her parents and ask them for her number—but it's a tough day for them, too, and I don't want to drag up bad memories for them. I could wait until my lunch-break and just drop by her flat, but...' He shook his head. 'I just need to call Natalie and see if she's OK.'

'I see.' Lenox looked thoughtful.

'I know it's against the rules. But sometimes rules need

to be bent, to—' Oh, no. Wrong tack. He didn't want Lenox thinking that there was any question over Tally's suitability for the position of house officer or future progression in her career. She was going to make a superb doctor, and Kit wasn't going to put obstacles in her way. 'Look, I'm not saying she'd do anything stupid. She's far too sensible for that. But I just know how she'll be feeling today.' The same way he felt. Empty. Bleak. Still railing against the fate that had ripped their lives apart. Wishing, wishing, wishing to hell that things were different. 'So I need to talk to her, to make sure she's all right. Please?'

The moments dragged by. Finally, Lenox nodded. 'As the circumstances are exceptional, I'll bend the rules this once. And I won't mention what you told me to anyone, even Natalie.'

'Thank you,' Kit said quietly.

Lenox took a file from his cabinet, looked up Natalie's record and wrote the number on a piece of paper for Kit.

'I appreciate this,' Kit said.

'Give her my best when you speak to her,' Lenox said. 'And tell her, if she needs to talk about things at any time, I'm here.'

Just like Kit hadn't been.

And then he noticed the photograph on Lenox's desk. Three children—the eldest sitting, the middle one standing and the baby on the eldest one's lap. Even now, Kit knew that his consultant would be thinking about his children. Realising how lucky he'd been. And Kit would just bet that all three children would get an extra-big hug from their father when he got home from his shift.

He didn't wait for his break, he simply went outside and rang Natalie from his mobile phone. There was no answer, as he'd half expected, but he didn't bother leaving a message on her machine. Maybe she'd gone to spend the day with her parents in Cotswolds.

Though somehow he doubted it. He had a feeling that it would be like Ethan's birthday. A day when she just wanted to be on her own. She was probably at the grave, laying fresh flowers there. But maybe she might share today with him. Ease the burden. Ease the heartache, the empty space inside.

As soon as Kit's shift finished, he drove to Litchford-in-Arden. He reached the churchyard while it was still just light enough to see where he was walking. There was no sign of Tally in the churchyard, but there were fresh roses on Ethan's grave, and a holly wreath.

A wreath for their son for Christmas, when he should have had a big red stocking with a furry white top. There should have been a glass of milk and a mince pie left out for Santa on Christmas Eve, with a carrot for the reindeer and a pile of wrapped presents under the tree on Christmas morning. Talcum-powder footprints, so their little boy would marvel that Santa had walked in from the 'snow'. Home-made decorations hanging on the tree from nursery and school, bells made from egg boxes covered in glitter with a loop of narrow tinsel.

Instead, there were flowers. Stupid bloody flowers.

How come it still hurt so much, every year?

And who was it who kept fostering the lie about time being a healer? As time passed, sure, a scab formed over the wound. But every anniversary stripped it raw again.

Kit didn't disturb Natalie's arrangement but left his flowers, still wrapped, lying on the grass in front of the wreath. 'God bless, my little boy. How I miss you,' he whispered. 'How I miss what we should have had. Our family.' He blinked to stop his eyes stinging, then headed back to his car.

It was a mistake to have the radio on. The classical station he'd tuned into was playing carols. An *a capella* version of 'In the Bleak Midwinter'.

Bleak didn't even begin to describe how he felt right now. Sitting the car in a church car park, in the twilight, on his own.

He switched off the radio and headed back to Birmingham. He parked at the side of the road where Natalie lived, then found her flat. She didn't answer the doorbell, but he'd seen her car parked further down the street. She was there all right, she just wasn't answering. Though he couldn't see any lights. Which meant she must be sitting there on her own, in the darkness.

He'd said to Lenox that Tally wouldn't do anything stupid. Had he been wrong about that? Was the weight of today so much that she'd…?

God, no. It didn't bear thinking about. He'd already programmed her number into his mobile phone; he pushed the button to dial it again. As he'd expected, the answering-machine kicked in. He grimaced as he listened to the message, then waited for the long beep. This time, he left a message. 'Tally, it's Kit. I know you're there—I can see your car. I'm worried about you. Just pick up the phone so I know you're OK and you haven't done anything that will make me kick your door down and drive you straight to the emergency department at St Joseph's. Please?'

No answer.

Fear blazed through him. Please, please, please, don't let her have done anything stupid. And why the hell had he let his pride get in the way? Why hadn't he bridged the gap between them, made her talk, made her understand that he was there for her? Why had he let her struggle on her own?

He hung up, and was about to put his shoulder to her door and break it down when the light came on and the door opened. Natalie stood there, her face white. In jeans, he registered, and an unironed long-sleeved T-shirt. Bare feet. As if it had been an effort for her even to get dressed that morning, a day when everything hurt too much.

'How did you get my number?' she demanded.

He'd invaded her privacy. Bad move. She clearly resented it. And he couldn't blame her. But all he could think about was the fact that she was OK. That she hadn't been driven completely over the edge. 'I bent a few rules because I was worried about you. I was going to come and see you anyway today.' He dragged in a breath. 'You look like hell.' And she was shivering.

'I can't stand today,' she whispered. 'It's the day of the year I just can't handle.'

The misery in her voice broke his heart. 'I know, honey, I know. It's bad for me, too.' At least he'd managed to block most of it out through work. She'd been on her own. She'd had time to think. Time to brood. Time to mourn their loss. He stepped forward and held her close, cradling her against his chest and stroking her hair.

And he was whispering to her, whispering the words he should have said all those years ago. 'It's going to be all right. I'm here. We'll get through this, honey. It's going to be all right, I promise.'

She shuddered against him, but her arms were wrapped tightly round him, as if she'd never let him go. The same way he was holding her. And he never, ever wanted to let her go again.

Somehow—he had no idea how—they were standing inside her flat and the front door was closed behind them. He rested his cheek against the top of her head, breathing in the clean scent of her hair. Thank God, she was letting him hold her. Letting him melt the frozen barriers between them with the warmth of his body.

As if she'd guessed his thoughts, she pulled back slightly and scrubbed at her face with the back of her hand. 'Sorry. I didn't—'

'Don't apologise,' he cut in gently. 'I'm the one person you can cry with today, if you need to. And I'm here, Tally. I'm *here*.'

Her flat was tiny. There were four doors leading off the hallway. He assumed one was her bedroom, one the bathroom and one the living room; through the open door, he could see her kitchen. A narrow, galley-type room with a table at one end. The light was on, so he'd been wrong: she hadn't been sitting in the dark. She must have had the door closed so he'd been unable to see the light.

'Come and sit down. I'll make you a hot drink,' he said softly.

He knew he was taking over. Bossing her about. Knew that in ordinary circumstances she'd be caustic about it and she wouldn't let him get away with it. But today wasn't ordinary. It was the darkest day of the year—not literally, as the winter solstice hadn't yet arrived—but this was the day of the year when it felt as if the sun didn't rise. When it felt as if the sun would never rise again.

Natalie allowed him to lead her into her kitchen, settle

her at the table. He hit lucky with the first cupboard door he opened—Tally had always kept the mugs and the coffee in the cupboard above the kettle, and her habits clearly hadn't changed. He made them both a mug of coffee, adding a spoonful of sugar and some milk to hers before bringing them over to the table.

She took one mouthful, and gagged. 'Ick. Sugar.'

'I know you don't take it normally. But I think you need it right now—I would've made you sweet tea, but I know you loathe it, and coffee's the next best thing.' He looked at her. 'Have you eaten at all today?'

She shook her head. 'I can't face anything.'

He knew what she meant. He'd only seen food as fuel today. Hadn't had a clue what he'd eaten. His sandwich at lunchtime could've been made from cardboard and he wouldn't have been able to tell the difference.

'Ah, honey.' He wanted to pull her onto his lap and comfort her, but he didn't dare go that far. 'Let me make you something. A sandwich.'

She shuddered. 'I can't. It'd be like swallowing ashes.'

'Tally, you have to eat. If you don't, low blood sugar's going to make you feel even worse.' In the old days, he remembered, her preferred comfort food had been cheese on toast. 'I'll make you something.' The activity made him feel better. And how weird it was—he'd never been in this room before, but he knew exactly where she kept everything. Bread in the china crock, cheese and tomatoes in the fridge, sharp knife in the cutlery drawer by the sink.

Just as it had been in their cottage in Litchford-in-Arden.

It didn't take long before the bread was toasted and the cheese was bubbling on top of the sliced tomatoes. He slid it onto a plate, cut each slice into four triangles, and brought the plate over to her.

'Just take a bite. One little bite. For me,' he encouraged.

She made a face, but she bit into one triangle. He watched her eat it, then another. But then she pushed the plate away, leaving most of it untouched. 'Sorry. I just…can't.'

'No worries.' He reached across the table and took her hand. 'I know how you're feeling. Same as me. Hollow inside.' A huge, empty space that couldn't be filled.

'I hate this time of year,' she said. 'I hate Christmas.'

He'd noticed that there were no decorations in the hall, no cards up, no holly wreath on the door. Tally had always decked their hall with boughs of holly, just like in the Christmas carol. She'd always had the cards on display, putting them up seconds after she'd scooped them up from the doormat. And they'd always had a real tree, filling the air with its scent. She'd even put together a stocking for him every year, filled with silly presents to make him laugh. The year they'd been totally broke, their first Christmas as a married couple, she'd wrapped up a packet of teabags in his stocking. Individually. And had made him guess what each little square parcel might contain. They'd laughed and laughed and fallen into bed, not caring.

Today, Natalie's Christmas cards were in a pile on the dresser. Not even a neat pile at that. As if she'd gone through the motions of opening them, but had lost all heart before she'd read half through the greeting.

'Celebrating the birth of a baby, just after the death of mine.' Her breath hitched. 'How can I do that?'

'I know.' He gave her a bleak smile. 'It's never been the same for me either—not since the year we got sympathy cards when we should've been celebrating our first Christmas as a family.'

The last word broke her. She propped her elbows on the table, buried her face in her hands and sobbed.

He couldn't just stay to the side and watch her. Couldn't stay apart. He shifted her chair back from the table, picked her up, sat down on her chair and settled her on his lap. Held her tight, stroking her hair and letting her howl into his chest until she'd cried herself back under control.

At last, she lifted her head. 'I'm—'

'Hurting,' he said, heading off her apology. God, he was the last person she needed to apologise to. If anything, he should be the one making the apologies. He stroked her face. 'It's better out than in.'

Ha. Said he, who'd always blocked out his feelings with work. Except for that moment in the churchyard, six weeks ago.

Her eyes were puffy and her face was hot. 'Hey. Stay here for a second,' he said, lifting her off his lap and settling her back onto the chair. He assumed the first two doors on the corridor would be her bedroom and living room, and when he opened the door to the bathroom he was relieved that he'd got it right.

There was a flannel folded neatly over the rim of the sink. He soaked it in cool water, squeezed it out then returned to the kitchen. Wiped her face, then laid the cool flannel over her eyelids, holding it there to relieve the swelling.

She lifted one hand, curled it over his. 'Why are you being so nice?' she whispered.

Because you're the love of my life and I hate to see you hurting. I want to make you feel better. Not that he was going to tell her that. It wasn't the right time. 'Because I care, Tally. Whatever's happened between us, I still care.' He still loved her. And he always would.

CHAPTER NINE

SOMEHOW—Kit couldn't even remember moving—he was sitting down, on his own chair this time, and Natalie was sitting on his lap. The damp flannel lay on the table, discarded. Her arms were round his neck, her fingers sliding into his hair. And he was kissing her eyelids, tiny butterfly kisses brushing down to the corners of her eyes, her temples. The lightest, lightest touch. A moth's wing against the candle flame.

And he was burning.

'Kit…'

But her voice wasn't saying 'stop'. It was saying 'go on'. That husky, slurring note he remembered from years ago. From the first time they'd made love, when he'd taken his time exploring her skin. When he'd found out just how and where she liked to be touched, where she liked to be kissed. What made her sigh with pleasure, what made her hyperventilate. What made her come apart in his arms.

There was a sensitive spot by her ear, he knew. And, just as he remembered, she reacted by giving a sharp intake of breath and tipping her head back. Offering him her throat. Her beautiful, beautiful throat.

It had always been so good between them. How could

he possibly resist? And right now he thought they both needed to reaffirm that they were still alive. He drew a trail of tiny, nibbling kisses down her throat to her collar-bone. Lord, her skin was so soft, so sweet.

He found her pulse beating strong and hard. He touched the tip of his tongue to it, marvelling at how her body still reacted to him. Even after all this time they were physically still in tune. Her hands were in his hair, and her fingertips were pushing hard against his scalp, urging him on—not that he needed much encouragement. He moulded his hands to her curves, sliding down until he found the hem of her T-shirt, then slipped his hands underneath and splayed his fingers flat against her bare midriff.

He wasn't sure who was shivering most—her or him. The sweet floral notes of her perfume and the scent of her skin were driving him crazy. He was burning up with need. He needed to touch, see, taste. Needed to be skin to skin with her. Needed her to touch him, to make him feel alive again.

As if she'd read his mind, she untucked his shirt and slid her hands under the soft cotton and along his back, smoothing along his musculature. He exhaled sharply at the first touch. Oh, it felt good, so good. Like sunshine beating down on his naked skin after half a lifetime of walking through the freezing rain.

And he wanted more. More. Much more.

He moved his hands higher, skating along the edge of her ribcage, and felt her gasp. So near, yet too far away. For both of them.

Kit moved his hands higher still to cup her breasts. The lace of her bra was flimsy, but it didn't hide her arousal. Her nipples were hard, and she shuddered as his thumbs grazed them through the lace. Her eyes were open but unfocused, the pupils huge with desire.

A desire he shared. More than shared.

Touching wasn't enough. He needed to see her—now. Taste her. He slid one hand around her back, fumbled with the clasp of her bra and heard her sharp sigh of relief echoing his mental one as the clasp finally gave way. She lifted her arms, letting him peel the T-shirt from her; her bra dropped to the floor at the same time, leaving her naked from the waist up.

Kit arched back for a moment just so he could look at her, drink in his fill.

Lord, she was beautiful. She was thinner than he remembered, her breasts smaller, but she was still gloriously curvy. Her skin was so pale, the perfect foil for her dark hair. He'd loved just looking at her, with those dark curls falling over her shoulders against her bare skin. Yet her new style, the short gamine cut, was just as sexy. Sophisticated.

He cupped her breasts, lifting them, feeling their warmth and weight. He wanted to tell her how gorgeous she was, how much he wanted to touch her and taste her and make love with her, but he couldn't speak—he was too full of longing and need for the words to come out.

Longing and need—and love.

He loved this woman with every fibre of his being. Always had. Always would. He'd been stupid enough to lose her six years ago. Now, please, please, let him find his way to her again. Build the first bridge between them. Show her with his body just how much he wanted her back in his life.

For good.

Slowly, slowly, Kit dipped his head. His mouth traced

the valley between her breasts, and then at last he drew one nipple into his mouth. Sucked. Licked. Teased it gently with his tongue and his teeth and his lips, until Natalie was quivering. Then he did it all over again with her other nipple.

'Oh-h-h.' Her gasp was soft and needy.

She was wearing way too much for his liking. So was he. And he couldn't wait any more. He wanted her now. He stopped playing with her breasts. Cupped her face. Touched his mouth to hers, and poured his soul into the kiss. Oh, please, let her understand how much he loved her, how much he regretted losing her, how much he wanted her back. Right now he couldn't frame the words. But he needed her to know this wasn't just sex. This wasn't just a need to reaffirm life on a day that was filled with sadness. And this definitely wasn't something he wanted to do with any other woman.

Only with Tally.

He kissed her until he was dizzy. And then he realised he wasn't wearing his jacket any more. Or his shirt. He had no idea which one of them had removed them or when— or even where they were—but it felt good, so good, to have Tally's hands on him again. Stroking his pecs, skating over his skin, her hands learning his shape all over again.

The tips of her fingers brushed against the soft hair on his chest, then followed the line down, down over his abdomen. When her fingers dipped just inside the waistband of his trousers, he shivered. Closed his eyes. God, he wanted this so much. Needed this.

He tipped his head back in offering and felt her mouth teasing his skin. He loved it when she kissed his throat like that. He loved feeling her mouth against his body. When she touched the tip of her tongue to the pulse beating frantically at the base of his throat, he knew she must be able to tell what effect she was having on him. How crazy she was driving him.

That, and the fact that she was straddling him. She'd be able to feel his erection pressing against her through her jeans, just as he could feel the heat of her sex against him. She'd know just how much she aroused him, how much he wanted her.

And it felt as if she wanted him just as much.

Please, don't let him be wrong about this.

'I need you, Tally,' he whispered. 'Now.'

'Yes,' she said, her voice equally soft and low.

He stood up, lifting her with him; she wrapped her legs round him.

'Tell me where to go,' he said softly. And, please, don't let it be 'to hell', he begged silently.

'Second door.'

Carrying her to her bed sent desire thrilling down his spine. He'd done this before. On the day she'd got her first-class honours degree in history. The day she'd passed her post-graduate course. The day he'd qualified as a doctor. Their wedding night, when he'd carried her over the threshold of the bridal suite that had been her parents' gift to them. And then again when they'd returned to their cottage in Litchford-in-Arden as a married couple—he'd carried her over the threshold of their home and straight to their bed.

Red-letter days that had been among the best in his life.

And maybe, just maybe, this was a return to those days. A new start. A chance to wipe out the bitterness and glory in the best of their love.

He laid her down gently on her bed. A double bed, he noticed with relief. He was way too old to try finessing his lover in a single bed. He and Tally had shared a single bed every night at university, sneaking in to each other's rooms and flouting the rules of the hall of residence which had decreed no visitors of the opposite sex after two a.m., but that felt like a lifetime ago.

Well, it was a lifetime ago—the days when he used to laugh a lot and all was right with his world because he'd wake up with the love of his life in his arms.

He'd missed her so much. Needed her so badly.

He clicked on her bedside light and closed the curtains.

She had to be crazy, Natalie thought. When Kit had asked her where to go, she should have told him to get out of her flat and out of her life.

But, oh, she'd missed him so much. And she was cold. So cold. Frozen to the bone. She needed his body heat to warm her, take the chill from her heart.

Just any man wouldn't do. She wanted Kit. Kit, who knew all her magic spots and whose mouth and hands could drive her crazy. Kit, who understood the way she was feeling right now—he felt the same way, probably—and could make her feel better.

They'd make each other feel better. Heal the hurt.

As Kit joined her on the bed, Natalie reached up to touch his face. There was a slight roughness under her fingertips, the beginnings of stubble. And he looked sexy as hell, his eyes dark with passion and his mouth slightly parted. Funny, even the shadows under his eyes made him look sexy. Dangerous.

'Ah, Kit.' She cupped his face, sat up, pressed her mouth against his.

His arms wrapped around her, holding her tight, and his mouth opened under hers. Letting her set the pace, she noticed. Not that he wasn't capable of taking over, taking control. But she liked the fact that he was putting her needs first.

And, oh, she was going up in flames.

Slowly, she leaned backwards until she was resting against the pillows and Kit was lying half on top of her, still kissing her. But it wasn't enough. She needed more. Needed to feel him inside her. Needed him to take her to another universe, a universe where it was just the two of them and the stars whirled dizzily round them.

She tilted her hips against him. She could feel just how hard he was, how much he wanted her—and she wanted him just as badly.

'Now,' she breathed. 'I need you inside me. Now.'

It took only seconds to strip each other of the rest of their clothes.

And that was it. No more barriers. Just the two of them. Skin to skin.

He nuzzled her cheek. 'Tally, this might not be as good as you deserve. I'm a bit out of practice,' he murmured.

Why should that please her so much? Selfish. Mean. Bitchy even. But she couldn't help hugging herself mentally. He hadn't tried to forget her in wild sex with a different woman every night. So what they'd shared had been special. It had meant something to him.

She slid her fingers down his spine. 'Doesn't matter.' And it was her turn to make a confession now. 'Know what? So am I.'

Both of them were in a mess. And maybe, just maybe, they could heal each other. Ease the pain. Find a way back to the sunlight.

'Just love me, Kit,' she whispered.

His gaze held hers, a deep, intense blue, then his hand slid between her thighs. Stroking, caressing, his clever fingers teasing her to the point where she thought she was going to spontaneously combust.

'O-h-h. I can't—I can't—Kit, *now*!' she begged.

He stole a kiss then, finally, he eased inside her. Filling her. Oh, Lord, it had been so long. So long. How could she have forgotten that it was like this between them?

He paused for a moment, waiting until her body had grown used to the feel of his again. And then he moved. Taking it slow and easy.

The magic was still there between them. The spark that had started on the dance floor at the fundraiser was now snapping and crackling and turning into a blaze. More than a blaze… A supernova. White heat, light, spinning round her. A feeling she hadn't had in years.

'Kit. Yes. Please. *Yes*,' she sighed, wrapping her legs around his waist and urging him deeper. Oh, it was good. So good. The way his body drove into hers, pushing her deeper and deeper into arousal. Heat radiated through her, from the soles of her feet to the tips of her fingers to the nerve-endings in her scalp.

How could she have forgotten how good this was, how amazing Kit made her feel?

It was like being in an oasis after years of wandering through a desert, lost and empty, Kit thought. And his mouth was filled with the sweetness of Tally's. He didn't think he'd ever be able to stop kissing her. Teasing her mouth, brushing her lips with his, until the tingling was too much to bear and he needed a deeper kiss, a hot, wet meeting of mouths that made his body scream for completion.

He'd almost forgotten how good this was. The warm sweetness of her body wrapped around his. The way his pulse rocketed. The feel of her heart beating against his, hard and fast. Urgent. The surge of his blood as his body thrust into hers. Her hands smoothing down his spine, cupping his buttocks, urging him deeper. Complete abandonment to the heat rising between them. The feeling that he could fly.

He felt Natalie's body begin to ripple around his; as he fell into his own release, he cried out her name. Natalie. His love, his life. His one and only.

When he rested his cheek against hers, it was wet. And he wasn't entirely sure whose silent tears they were.

Tally lay curled in Kit's arms, her head resting on his shoulder, his arm wrapped around her waist and her legs tangled with his. The way they'd always curled up together after making love. Just as if the past six years had never happened. As if they'd never been apart.

And then it sank in. What they'd just done.

Oh, Lord.

This shouldn't have happened. The sex had been amazing—it always had been good between them—but it just wasn't enough. It wasn't enough to keep a relationship together, and they couldn't go back to how things used to be. How things had been before Ethan.

And although Kit had been there for her today—had held her when she'd needed it, washed her face so tenderly when she'd stopped crying, looked after her, made her something to eat—how could she be sure he'd be there the next time she needed him? Hadn't he spent today at work after all, using work to block out his feelings?

Just as he'd done when Ethan had died.

So he hadn't changed. Not deep down.

And he hadn't said a word to her about how he felt. Not a single word. No 'I love you'. Nothing.

What man would refuse when he was offered sex on a plate? She'd virtually thrown herself at him, so of course he'd carried her to bed. She'd been such an idiot. Reading much more into it than was really there. Today they'd both been feeling low. Miserable. And having sex was the best way to reaffirm life, make you feel connected to someone. That was all this had been.

It was a mistake and it needed to stop.

Right here, right now.

Slowly, Natalie disentangled her legs from Kit's. Moved his arm from her waist. Wriggled out of his hold and shifted as far away as she could from him.

He turned to her, frowning. 'Tally? What's the matter?'

Did he really not know? 'We can't do this. We're divorced.'

He looked mystified, as if he didn't see what the problem was. 'There isn't a law against it.'

'That's not what I meant. This is all wrong.' Her mouth felt dry with misery. 'We're trying to turn back the clock, pretend nothing's happened, and we can't. This was a mistake. We—we shouldn't have done this.' Her breath shuddered. 'I think you should go.'

'Tally…' He reached out to her, but she shrank away.

She didn't trust herself. If she let him hold her, she knew what would happen next. They'd never been able to get enough of each other's bodies. One touch, and they'd be making love again. And although her body was desperate to be close to Kit's again, her head was shrieking all kinds of warnings. This was all wrong, wrong, wrong. It had to stop now.

'Please. Just go.'

He flinched, as if she'd just slapped him. Hard. And then his face went completely blank. 'If that's what you want,' he said, his voice carefully neutral. 'Perhaps you wouldn't mind looking away while I find my clothes.'

Tally closed her eyes in shame and misery. His clothes. God only knew where they were. Where hers were. Tangled in a heap, strewn all over her flat? She and Kit had been so desperate for each other, neither of them had cared where their clothes landed when they'd stripped each other. He'd carried her to bed, and they'd both been so crazy with desire and need, nothing had had mattered any more.

And now they were going to have to face the consequences.

What a mess. What a bloody, bloody mess. They'd made love. And he had been so, so sure they'd broken down some of the barriers between them. That maybe, just maybe, there was a chance for them to right past wrongs. Talk it through. Understand each other. And then they could wipe the slate clean—forgive each other and start again.

Tally clearly didn't feel the same way.

The words 'I love you' had died on Kit's lips before he could say them. They'd withered away from the look on her face, when she'd shrunk from his touch.

This was a mistake.

Yes, there'd been a mistake all right. And clearly it had been all his.

Grimly, he climbed out of bed and found his boxer shorts and trousers in a heap on the floor. Dragged them on. He went hunting for his shirt, jacket and tie, and finally found them in the kitchen. Discarded on the floor. Crumpled and uncared for.

Yeah, he knew how that felt all right.

He finished dressing. Shoved his tie in his pocket. Slipped on his shoes. Tally hadn't reappeared—well, her clothes were all over the place, too, and she was probably too embarrassed to come out from her bedroom naked. Then again, there were such things as dressing-gowns. And her wardrobe was in her bedroom. The fact she hadn't emerged at all told him she was staying in bed, not wanting to face him. Clearly she didn't want to face what they'd just done. Didn't want to talk to him at all.

Well, that was fine by him. Right now he didn't particularly want to talk to her either. Gritting his teeth, he walked out of her flat. Closed the door behind him. And as the lock clicked, he heard all his hopes shatter.

CHAPTER TEN

KIT spent a sleepless night. Every time he closed his eyes, he saw Natalie flinching away from him. And it made him ache like hell. Did she really think he'd ever do anything to hurt her?

OK, yes, he could admit he'd got it wrong in the past. He hadn't been there for her when she'd needed him most. He'd shut her out—shut everyone out, really. But he'd grown up. Changed.

All he wanted was a second chance.

And she wasn't going to give it to him.

By morning, Kit's head was throbbing. Especially as he'd remembered something. Something he really needed to talk to her about. Something she really, really wasn't going to like. But they would have to be responsible and face it. Together.

He took some paracetamol to deal with his headache and headed for the ward. Thankfully, Lenox had switched the rosters so Kit was working in the PAU and Natalie was doing a ward round with the consultant. Just as well: he didn't think he could face working with her today. Not after the way she'd rejected him so absolutely yesterday.

'Is everything OK?' Lenox asked quietly before Kit headed for clinic.

No. Far from it. But Kit summoned a smile. 'Nothing to worry about,' he lied.

'Good.' Lenox didn't look entirely convinced, but to Kit's relief the consultant didn't press it.

Kit's first case was Nina, a teenager whose mother was convinced she was having a heart attack. 'She's got this pain in her chest,' Nina's mother said.

Nina, Kit noted, was white-faced with pain, but clearly didn't want to admit there was a problem. 'I'm all right, Mum. Stop fussing. And I'm going to get into trouble for missing school.'

'Can you tell me anything about the pain?' Kit asked.

'I'm all right,' Nina said, clearly not liking the fuss. 'My chest feels a bit tight, that's all.'

'You were nearly crying in pain when you sneezed this morning,' Nina's mother cut in.

Tight chest, pain. Oh, yes. Kit knew all about that—except his was mental rather than physical in origin.

A problem with Nina's heart was a possibility. He needed to rule out a few things. And, since she wasn't going to be that forthcoming, he'd have to prompt her to describe the pain. 'Is it a sharp pain, or a feeling as if someone's squeezing you?'

'A sharp pain,' she said.

So far, so good. 'Do you have pain anywhere else?' he asked, carefully making sure he didn't lead the teenager to an answer about pain radiating down her arm. If she said it of her own accord, he'd order further investigations—an electrocardiogram being the first one, to check the rhythm of her heart.

'No. It just hurts here.' She indicated an area a hand's breadth down from her collarbone on the left side.

Probably not a heart attack. 'How's your breathing?' he asked.

She shrugged, then winced as if the movement had caused her pain. 'Fine.'

'Any history of asthma—either you personally or someone else in the family?'

'No, nothing like that.'

OK. Time to rule out a few more things. 'May I listen to your heart?' he asked.

She nodded, and he checked her heartbeat: no sounds he didn't like. No murmurs, no unusual noises. That was a good sign. 'Breathe in for me. And out. And in. And out.' No crackles or wheezing either, so it wasn't a respiratory infection or asthma. He was beginning to have a pretty good idea of what the problem was. 'I think the problem might be with your ribcage. May I examine you?' At her nod, he gently worked his way down her ribs. 'Here's the first rib—just under your collar-bone. Second. Third.'

'Ow!'

Bingo. Just what he'd been expecting. And in exactly the right place, too.

'OK, Nina. It's tender around your second and third ribs, so I'm not going to press any further. What you have is a condition called costochondritis—that's an inflammation of the cartilage that connects the inner end of your ribs with your breastbone,' Kit explained, indicating on himself exactly the places he meant. 'Because of the swelling, it will tend to hurt when you move, or when you cough or sneeze.'

'Is it serious?' Nina's mother asked, looking worried.

He smiled at her. 'The good news is, no. It can be scary,

because most people's thought about a sharp pain in the chest is that it's a heart attack. About one in ten people get this kind of inflammation, and it's more common in young adults like Nina. It'll clear up of its own accord in a few weeks—in the meantime, you'll need to take painkillers to help you manage it,' he said to Nina. 'Have you taken anything for it yet?'

'Mum gave me some paracetamol but they didn't do a lot,' she said, grimacing.

'Start with ibuprofen,' he said. 'As well as being a pain-killer, it's an anti-inflammatory so it'll help to bring the swelling down a bit. If it doesn't seem to do much, make an appointment to see your GP for something a little stronger. It should clear up in a couple of weeks, but if it doesn't you might need a corticosteroid injection to bring down the inflammation and ease the pain. I'll be sending your doctor a note to say I've seen you and what my diagnosis is, but in the meantime you need to get plenty of rest and try to avoid any sudden movements.'

Right now, Kit thought, he'd welcome a physical pain he could deal with. Because the pain in his heart was killing him. Emotional pain. And there was nothing—absolutely nothing—he could take for it.

When he finished clinic, he went in search of Natalie. She was with a patient. 'Sorry for interrupting,' he said to the woman Natalie had been talking to. 'When you've finished, could we have a word in my office, Dr Wilkins?'

She looked strained, but nodded.

He headed for his office to catch up on paperwork following his clinic. The seconds dragged by, and still she didn't appear. Did that mean she was really busy, or did it mean she was avoiding him?

Just when he was about to save his file and go back to the ward to track her down, there was a knock at his door.

'Come in.'

To his relief, it was Natalie.

'Thanks for coming. Would you mind closing the door behind you?'

She looked faintly worried. Oh, for goodness' sake, did she think he was about to leap on her? 'Leave it open if you feel more comfortable. It doesn't really make any difference.'

She blushed. Good. She'd taken the point, then. She left the door open—as if making a point of her own—and took the chair he'd indicated.

'We need to talk,' he said softly.

'I don't think so.'

He raked a hand through his head. 'Tally, I really need to talk to you about something. But not here.' Even if she'd closed the door, he still wouldn't have broached the subject here. Not when there was such a likelihood of being inter-rupted. 'Have lunch with me. Not in the canteen—some-where quiet.'

'Quiet?' She raised an eyebrow. 'We're hardly going to find somewhere quiet at this time of year. All the restau-rants are full of people having Christmas parties, and all the cafés are full of Christmas shoppers.'

Yes, and he didn't want to have to yell what he wanted to say in the hubbub of a crowded room. 'OK, just you and me in the hospital gardens, then. I don't want to discuss this in front of other people.'

She frowned. 'Discuss what? There's nothing to say. We both agreed that yesterday was a mistake.'

He was too weary to argue. 'Tally, don't fight with me.

Please. Just meet me at…' he glanced at his watch '—a quarter to one by the main entrance. It won't take long.'

For a moment, he thought she was going to refuse. Then she sighed. 'All right. I'll see you at a quarter to one.'

Kit spent the rest of his morning catching up with paperwork—and he was relieved that he had something he had to concentrate on, so he could shut out the turmoil in his heart. Just for a little while.

At twenty to one, he was waiting outside the main entrance. He was glad it wasn't raining. He really, really needed the fresh air. Five minutes later—dead on time—Natalie walked out to join him.

'Let's walk,' he said softly, gesturing towards a bench underneath the bare trees in the far corner of the hospital gardens.

They walked in silence to the bench—a silence that grew tighter and tighter as they walked—and sat down.

'So what's this about?' she asked.

'Last night. We got…' Ah, hell. He'd practised the words in his head. But however he tried to put it, it sounded bad. 'We got carried away.'

'And it was a mistake,' Natalie cut in immediately.

She really, really wasn't going to like this. Especially because it looked as if it hadn't yet crossed her mind. 'Neither of us was thinking clearly. There might be consequences.'

She shook her head. 'I'm not with you.'

He sucked in a breath. Countdown to Tally going nuclear. 'We didn't use any contraception.'

She looked at him in utter horror as the penny clearly dropped. 'Oh, my God!'

He winced. 'If it makes you feel any better, I don't sleep around so you don't have to worry about catching an STD from me. I've had two relationships since we split up. Both of them were a fair while ago.' And neither of them had lasted long. He hadn't wanted them to: although the women concerned had both been lovely, sweet and kind, neither of them had been Natalie. Neither of them had made him feel the way Natalie made him feel. And it wouldn't have been fair to string them along.

'I don't sleep around either.' Her face was white. 'Last night was my first time since…'

His stomach dropped as he realised what she meant. Last night had been the first time she'd made love since having a baby.

There really hadn't been anyone since him.

They'd decided to wait until her six-week postnatal check-up before making love again after Ethan's birth. They'd touched each other, but not had full intercourse. And Natalie had missed her six-week check-up because Ethan had been in hospital. Afterwards, there had been a cold wall between them, and she'd moved into the spare room. Sex had been completely out of the equation. And then she'd walked out on him.

There had been nobody since him. So did that mean there was hope after all? Or was he just deluding himself, finding excuse after excuse not to face the fact that it was completely over between them?

Natalie folded one leg over the other and drummed her fingers on her knees, clearly calculating the date of her last period. 'We're probably OK. My last period started a week ago. You know as well as I do there's only a short window for fertility—days ten to fourteen—and the average couple trying for a baby has a one in four chance of conceiving during that window.'

True enough—but only to a certain extent. 'There's no such thing as a safe time, Tally. Ovulatory patterns aren't always consistent. Even if your monthly cycle's regular—' and it always had been, in the years they'd been together '— you get the odd month when things aren't the same. This might be your odd month. You might be pregnant.'

She gritted her teeth. 'We can't have made a baby, Kit. Not on the anniversary of Ethan's death. We *can't*.'

It wasn't so much making a baby that was freaking her, then—it was the timing. Even so. He was going to do the right thing. 'We probably haven't,' he reassured her. 'But if we have, I'll—'

'Just do what you did last time,' she cut in. 'Bury your head in the sand. Shut everything out except work.'

Ouch. He deserved that. But it wasn't entirely fair. 'You're the one who moved into the spare room, Tally. The evening Ethan died.' And he'd needed her to hold him so badly. Except she'd closed the door on him, claiming she had a headache and needed some sleep. He'd tried to put her needs first instead of being selfish and demanding that she return to the marital bed. He'd given her some space.

And what a mistake that had been. The beginning of the end.

'Then you left, without even talking to me about it first. You just wrote me a note saying you wanted a divorce, packed your bags and walked out on me.'

She glared at him. 'You didn't exactly try hard to get me back. Did you call me at my parents'? Did you say you loved me and wanted me to come home?'

No and no and no. Though he had loved her. Deeply.

'You didn't contest the divorce.'

'I was grieving, too,' he pointed out. 'I couldn't cope

with what was happening to us. And neither of us was offered grief counselling at the time. Neither of us dealt with it properly. We probably still haven't, if the truth be known.' He raked a hand through his hair. 'Tally, I admit was young and stupid back then. Things are different now.'

'Are they?'

'Yes. We're both older. Wiser.'

'That's as maybe. It doesn't change a thing.' She stood up. 'I'm going back to work.'

If she refused to discuss it, there wasn't much he could do about it. He could hardly force her to sit down and listen. Even if he did, she could tune him out. Do the mental equivalent of sticking her fingers in her ears and calling, 'La, la, I can't hear you.' He shrugged. 'As you wish. But, Tally, if you're pregnant, I'll stand by you. It's not optional.'

Her jaw tightened. 'I don't *want* you to stand by me.'

Oh, no. No way was he going to let her have his child and be shut out of both their lives. He'd lost one child. He couldn't bear to lose a second. 'If you're pregnant, it'll be my baby too.'

Then he saw a tear slide down her cheek. And he felt like the lowest form of life. She was crying—because he'd pushed her too hard. Made her deal with something she really wasn't ready to face.

Or maybe he hadn't pushed her far enough.

Right now he had no idea what was the right thing, what was the wrong thing. He just had to act on his gut instinct, and hope it wasn't steering him in the wrong direction. He reached out and took her hands. 'Tally. Talk to me,' he said softly. That was where they'd gone wrong last time. They hadn't talked, hadn't shared, had tried to deal with it alone instead of together. Maybe this was their chance to get it right.

'I can't.' She shook her hands free. 'Leave me alone, Kit. Please. I can't handle this.'

He heard the note of panic in her voice. Oh, hell. If he pushed her much further, she might break down completely—which wouldn't help either of them. It was time to back off, give her some space. Though this time he'd be careful not to leave it too long. He didn't want that wall going back up between them. He dragged in a breath. 'OK. I won't push it. But let me know if… I need to know, Tally.'

'If—and it's unlikely,' she pointed out, '*if* there's anything to tell you about, I'll let you know.'

And then she was walking away.

Kit watched her, biting his lower lip. It had been a mess to start with, and now it felt as if things were ten times worse. How the hell was he going to fix this? How was he going to prove to Natalie that he'd changed, that he wouldn't let her down again? How could he prove that he loved her?

So many questions. But, right then, he had no answers.

If anyone on the ward noticed over the next few days that Kit and Tally were avoiding each other as much as possible, they didn't say anything. Kit noticed that Lenox had switched the rosters round so he wasn't working with Tally—at her request maybe? He didn't know. And he couldn't ask. All he knew was that he went up in flames every time he saw her. He couldn't sleep, couldn't think straight.

And he really couldn't carry on like this.

If she wasn't going to give him another chance, then he

had to leave. After Christmas, he'd start applying for another job. Something that would take him a long, long way away from Tally. Maybe a secondment abroad.

A baby. They might have made a *baby*. Natalie hadn't even stopped to think—she'd just needed Kit. Needed to make love with him.

She'd acted like a sex-crazed lunatic. And then she'd thrown him out. Talk about giving mixed signals. No wonder he was avoiding her—he probably thought she was crazy.

Maybe she was.

All she knew was that she couldn't sleep. That she was aware of every time he walked onto the ward, whether she could see him or not. And that she really, really wasn't handling this well.

And if her period didn't start on Christmas Day…

No. It just didn't bear thinking about.

A few days later, Kit was walking down the corridor to his office when he heard a soft voice he knew well in one of the side rooms. Natalie was reading a story to one of their patients—Kyra, a six-year-old who'd recently been diagnosed with acute lymphoblastic leukaemia and was in for chemotherapy treatment. She'd become a favourite on the ward, and even those who weren't rostered as her designated nurse or doctor stopped by her bed for a chat or to read her a story.

Kyra was on her third week of the intensive first phase of treatment, and she'd been very brave throughout. Her parents had taken her to their GP with a high temperature, and the GP had noticed how pale the little girl was. When Kyra's mother had mentioned how easily Kyra seemed to bruise and how tired and lethargic she'd been, the GP had been on red alert and taken a blood sample before referring her to the ward. By the time she'd got to Nightingale Ward, Kyra had developed petechiae—flat, reddish pinhead spots on her skin—and on examination her lymph nodes, liver and spleen had been enlarged.

The blood tests had showed an elevated white cell count. Lenox had ordered a bone-marrow biopsy, which had confirmed presence of 'blasts', immature white cells that overcrowded the bone marrow and stopped it producing normal blood cells.

The cytotoxic drugs Kyra was taking to destroy the leukaemia cells had caused her hair to start falling out and she often felt nauseous, but she always had a smile for any visitors.

And she'd particularly taken to Tally. Kit was aware that Tally often lingered after her shift or skipped her lunchbreak to read to Kyra, and today was clearly no exception. She was reading a story about Christmas wishes.

Ha. He knew what his wish was. One that definitely wouldn't be granted.

'Dr Tally, are Christmas wishes special?' Kyra asked.

'They are. And sometimes they come true just when you think they won't,' Natalie said. 'Are you going to make a Christmas wish?'

'Yes. That I'll be home for Christmas and my mummy will smile again.'

'That's a lovely wish,' Natalie said.

'Will it come true?'

There was a long pause. 'We'll see what Santa can do.'

They were all hoping that Kyra could go home, even if it was only for Christmas Day. The intensive treatment took between four and six weeks and, depending on whether the bone-marrow biopsy showed the leukaemia was in remission or not, she might need to have a lumbar puncture with an injection of methotrexate directly into her spinal fluid. If that didn't work, radiotherapy was a possibility, and perhaps also a bone-marrow transplant, depending on how she responded to treatment. They all had their fingers crossed that she'd go into remission and stay there.

'What about your wish, Dr Tally?' Kyra asked.

Kit knew that he was eavesdropping on a private conversation. That he should walk on. Right now.

But he couldn't have moved if his life had depended on it.

Did Tally have a Christmas wish?

'I've got two wishes,' Natalie said softly. 'One of them isn't really a proper wish because I know it can't happen.' She coughed. 'So my real Christmas wish is that everyone on the ward has a very, very happy Christmas.'

One of them isn't really a proper wish because I know it can't happen.

Kit could guess what it was. That their baby hadn't died. But if Ethan hadn't died, the chances were that their marriage wouldn't have died either. They'd still be together now. So did Tally regret it just as much as he did? And did that mean that his own Christmas wish—that they'd have another chance at happiness—had a chance of being granted?

Maybe, Kit thought. Maybe.

And a flicker of hope lit the shadows around his heart.

A few minutes later, there was a knock on his door.

'Come in,' he called.

Natalie leaned round the edge of his door. 'Have you seen Lenox anywhere?'

Kit shook his head. 'It's his daughter's nativity play this afternoon. He won't be back until tomorrow. Anything I can help with?'

Natalie looked at him for a moment, as if weighing him up, then nodded. 'Kyra. What are the chances of her going home for Christmas Day?'

'Not high.' He sighed heavily. 'Yes, it'd be a lovely gesture and it would probably perk her up no end. But you know as well as I do that the drugs she's on reduce the number of blood cells produced by the bone marrow, meaning that she's at much greater risk of picking up an infection. All it needs is for someone visiting her to be going down with a cold, and she'll become one very sick little girl.'

'But if her parents could make sure she didn't come into contact with anyone who had a cold or even the faintest sniffle, couldn't she go home? Just for a couple of hours? Let her feel as if it's a normal Christmas?'

'A couple of hours would be better than a whole day,' Kit said. 'Let me have a look at her file. I'll review it—and if I think the benefits outweigh the risks, I'll plead your case with Lenox.' He might not be able to make Tally's Christmas wish come true, but maybe he could give their patient a special present. Her Christmas wish. A chance to go home.

CHAPTER ELEVEN

LATER that week, Lenox was speaking at a conference in Bristol, leaving Kit as acting consultant for the day. Kit came in for his shift an hour early so he could run through the handover from the night staff. And when he heard a hacking cough and noisy breathing in the corridor outside his office, he sighed. It sounded like another case of bronchiolitis. This would be the sixth in two days. At this time of year the illness—a lower respiratory tract infection condition where the very small airways in the lungs became inflamed—was virtually an epidemic among children under the age of one. Right now Nightingale Ward had a whole bay of infants being barrier-nursed with 'RSV+' written on the boards outside their rooms to show that their nasal swabs had shown positive for respiratory syncitial virus.

It was always very upsetting for the parents, seeing their babies being fed through a nasogastric tube and with an oxygen mask on. He'd been there himself, knew how bad it felt. How hopeless you felt, how frustrated that you couldn't do anything to save your baby any pain. All you could do was sit beside the bed or crib, maybe hold their hands and talk to them so they knew you were there with them. And it never felt as if you were doing enough.

Kit walked out of his office, about to introduce himself to the parents and add a bit of extra reassurance that although all the tubes and wires looked frightening they really didn't hurt—feeding the baby through a nasogastric tube meant that he or she didn't get tired, the oxygen made it a lot easier for the baby to breathe, and the pulse oximeter meant they could keep an eye on the baby's pulse and oxygen saturation levels—when he realised that it wasn't a patient coughing. It was Natalie.

'You sound terrible. What on earth are you doing here?' he asked, folding his arms. 'You should be at home, off sick.'

'I'm OK.'

She could barely get the words out. Had to take a dragging breath between words. And her voice was little more than a whisper.

Ah, hell. Sometimes he really hated her stubborn streak. 'Tally, go home.'

'On duty.' Breath. 'Not…' Pause. 'Your place…' dragging breath '…to tell me…' Pause. 'What to do.'

How the hell did she expect to get through her shift in this sort of state? His mouth compressed. 'Actually, it is. Lenox is giving a paper, so I'm acting consultant today. And you definitely shouldn't be here. Apart from the fact you're not well enough to work, this is a paediatric ward. Kids have lower immune systems than adults in any case, and the last thing they need is to get this virus on top of the one they've already got. Especially patients like Kyra.'

He noticed her flinch at the word 'virus'. Thinking of Ethan, no doubt. Or maybe feeling guilty at the fact that she hadn't put their patients first. Especially as they'd had that conversation about why Kyra might not be allowed home for Christmas, the risk of her contracting a virus being too high.

'Come with me,' he said, taking her arm.

'What?'

'Don't argue with me, Tally. It's hard enough for you to breathe as it is, without you getting agitated and making it worse. Just come with me.' He marched her into his office, locked his door and pulled the blind. 'Take your white coat off, and lift up your top. Now.'

She made a noise of outraged protest.

Oh, for goodness' sake! Did she think he was making some kind of clumsy, unsubtle pass at her? She should know him well enough to realise that wasn't his style. If he wanted her to take her clothes off, he'd just let the heat between them work for him.

Though he had no intention of doing that either. Last time they'd done that, it had made things even more awkward between them. There was no point in making it worse still.

He waved his stethoscope at her. 'It sounds as if you've got a chest infection, Natalie. Knowing you, you won't make an appointment with your GP to get it checked out—and this time of year you'd be lucky to get an appointment anyway. So you may as well get checked out here. On the ward. By a qualified doctor.'

She flushed, clearly realising she'd misread his intentions. Good. Perhaps now she'd listen to him—where her health was concerned, at any rate.

'Now, lift up your top so I can listen to your chest.'

She said nothing and submitted to the examination.

'Breathe in. And out. And in. And out.' He frowned. 'OK, I'm going to take a listen at the back. Breathe in. And out. And again.' He paused. 'OK, you can put your top down again now.'

She looked near to tears, and he had to fight the urge to drag her into his arms and tell her everything was going to be all right. 'Your chest is clear—no wheezing or crackles—so it's viral and not bacterial. I'm not going to write you a scrip for antibiotics because they won't clear this up any faster, but you're really not in a fit state to work. Look at yourself. You've got no colour, there are dark smudges under your eyes and you're having trouble breathing.' He gave her a grim smile. 'I'll spare you the nasal swab on condition you go home right now and stay in bed for a couple of days.'

'OK.'

The fact she was so docile about it really had him worried. She must be feeling seriously rough. He made a snap decision. 'You're not fit to drive yourself. I'll take you.'

'You're on duty. Can't. I'll get a taxi.'

Each word was clearly an effort between coughs, and her breathing was laboured. He really, really didn't like this. She probably would get a taxi—but she'd be going home to an empty flat, where he very much doubted she'd look after herself properly. He'd already noticed how bare her fridge had been, when he'd made her the cheese on toast. And she'd lost weight over the last week, too. What with the upset of this time of year and the pressure he'd put her under, she probably hadn't been eating properly, and her immune system had lowered to the point where she was an easy victim for a virus.

'Tally, don't argue. I'm taking you home.' He buzzed through to the nurses' desk. To his relief, the senior sister answered. 'Just the woman I need. Debbie, can you do me a favour, please, honey?'

'Sure.'

'Can you get onto the bank team for me? I need a locum for Natalie for the next week.'

'Has she got that awful chest bug that's going round?'

'Yes. And she's really not fit to drive, so I'm taking her home. I'll be an hour, tops. Call my mobile if it's urgent. If I'm not driving, I'll answer; if I am, I'll pull into the next safe place and call you back.'

'OK, Kit.'

'Thank you, Debbie.' He replaced the phone and looked at Tally. 'Coat, handbag—anything else you need from the staffroom?'

She shook her head.

'Right. We're going. Now.'

He set off at his usual pace and she matched him stride for stride, but halfway down the corridor he noticed she was coughing badly. Clearly the effort of walking was making her breathing more laboured and her cough worse. And when she clapped her hand to her mouth he stopped, delved in his pocket and brought out a clean handkerchief. 'Spit.'

'Nuh.' She grimaced as best as she could with what looked like a mouthful of phlegm.

He sighed. 'Tally, if you're coughing up stuff, don't swallow it because it will make the infection worse. You know that—you're a doctor.' And didn't they just make the worst patients? he thought grimly. 'The hankie can go in the wash, or the bin. I don't care. Just spit the stuff out.'

She scowled, but did as he asked. And he slowed his pace so breathing was easier for her. Waited for her in the staffroom while she got her stuff from the locker. Shepherded her to the car park and helped her into his car. Drove her back to his flat.

'Wrong…' cough '…way,' Tally whispered.

'Don't talk. Concentrate on breathing. Take it nice and slowly.' He parked outside his flat.

'Wrong—' she began.

'Tally, I said I was taking you home,' he cut in gently. 'I didn't say *your* home. You need someone to look after you right now. And that someone would be me. So I've brought you to my flat, and I'm going to keep an eye on you until you're better. Don't argue.' He opened the door, ushered her in, then marched her straight into his bedroom. He switched on the bedside light, closed the curtains, then rummaged in his wardrobe for a T-shirt to act as a makeshift nightie. Neither of them had bothered wearing anything in bed in the years they'd been together, but right now he knew that Natalie needed her dignity. His T-shirt would do just fine. 'Put that on and get into bed. I'll be back in a minute.'

'But—'

'Just get into bed, Tally,' he said, and left the room.

Natalie felt too ill to argue; her energy had completely deserted her. The only thing she wanted to do right now was curl up in a ball and sleep for a month. She stripped and pulled Kit's T-shirt on, then climbed into his king-sized bed and pulled the duvet up. The virus had temporarily wiped out her sense of smell, but she knew Kit's scent would be all around her. She was lying in his bed, between sheets he'd slept in. Wearing his T-shirt. And it was almost as if he were holding her, comforting her.

She rubbed the back of her hand across her eyes. She was not going to cry. Whatever was the matter with her? She wasn't normally this pathetic.

She heard a rap on the door. Kit. Preserving her modesty. Ha. Considering how many times he'd seen her naked…

And it made her want to cry even more. Because he was cherishing her. Thinking of her feelings. Putting her first.

'OK,' she rasped.

He was carrying a tray, which he slid onto the cabinet beside the bed. 'Hot honey and lemon. Your throat's sore, yes?'

She nodded.

'There are some throat lozenges here. Don't take more than one every three hours. But I've done you a jug of lemon barley water to keep you going in between. It's weak, so it won't hurt your throat, and it's iced so it'll stay cool during the day. Sip it slowly—if you gulp it, you'll bring it back up. If you run out, I've left the bottle out on the kitchen worktop. Help yourself. Ice is in the top drawer of the freezer.' He looked at her. 'But I'd rather you stayed put and got some rest. If you must, you can lie on the sofa and watch TV or a film, but you do *not* get up properly, understand? You take the duvet with you and you stay put.'

Bossy. She couldn't remember Kit being this bossy. Except maybe when she'd been pregnant with Ethan and he'd turned into a paid-up member of the food police, making sure there were no raw eggs or unpasteurised dairy foods in anything she ate.

Weirdly, she liked it.

The virus must have addled her brains. She was an independent woman, perfectly capable of doing things for herself. She didn't need anyone to look after her.

'I've made you some lunch,' he added.

Lunch. She glanced at the tray. A sandwich with the crusts cut off and covered in cling film so the bread wouldn't go hard with curled edges before she could eat it. A bowl of grapes. A tangerine, which he'd peeled and segmented—and he'd even removed all the white pith. And he'd rustled up a box of tissues from somewhere.

He was making a serious fuss of her.

Now she really wanted to cry.

'If there's nothing there you fancy, have a rummage in the fridge.' He looked at her for a moment. 'I'll be straight home after my shift. But if you need anything, you know the ward's number. Call me.' He gestured to his bedside table. 'The phone's right here.' He took her hand and squeezed it briefly. 'Now, get some rest, OK?'

He scooped up her clothes, and she frowned. 'Where?' she croaked.

He must have guessed the rest of her question because his eyes crinkled at the corners. 'I'm putting your clothes in the washing machine—just in case you had any mad ideas about waiting until I'd gone back to work, then getting dressed, calling a taxi and going back to your place.' This time there was a definite quirk to his lips. 'Even *you* can't go anywhere in soaking wet clothes.'

She pulled a face at him.

'I'm looking after you until you're better, Tally, whether you like it or not.'

She knew when she was beaten, and leaned back against the pillows.

'Rest,' Kit said. He smiled at her, and left.

It was a while before she heard the front door click—obviously he hadn't been joking about putting her clothes in the wash. Ha. If she'd felt better, she wouldn't have let him bully her into going to bed in the first place. She'd never been the sort to let a cold get the better for her. But right now she didn't have the energy to move, let alone go back to her flat.

Kit rang her twice to see how she was—once during his morning break and once during his lunch-break. And when Natalie heard his key in the door later, she was shocked to realise just how much she was looking forward to seeing him.

This was bad. Really bad. They weren't together any more. And she'd blown any chance of reconciliation when she'd panicked the night he'd made love with her again. When she'd thrown him out. When she'd refused to discuss anything with him the next day. When she'd freaked at the idea of having made another baby with him after they'd forgotten to use contraception.

She really didn't deserve his kindness now.

He rapped on the door. Observing her privacy and respecting it, she noticed.

'Come in,' she croaked.

'How are you doing?' He came to sit on the edge of the bed and laid his hand on her forehead. 'Hmm, you've got a bit of a temperature. I'll get you some paracetamol.'

''M OK,' she said, lifting her chin.

'No, you're not. Stop being brave. Some of these bugs are really nasty and I bet you feel terrible.' His hand slid down to cup her face for a moment, and his thumb brushed her cheek—as if he were soothing a fretful child.

'It's a bit like when you first started teaching—you pick up the bugs that go round the school. When you first start in paediatrics, you're exposed to viruses you wouldn't come across in normal circumstances, and more of them, so you're more vulnerable at first. Don't think of it as a weakness. You're doing the right thing by staying put, because you're not spreading it.' He stood up. 'Right. Paracetamol. And I'll get you a fresh drink.' He looked at her tray. She'd made an effort with the sandwich but she hadn't managed to force much of it down. 'Does it hurt to eat?'

'A bit,' she admitted.

'OK. I'll do you something soft for dinner.' He handed her the carrier bag she hadn't noticed him bring into the room. 'You never sit still, so I imagine boredom's starting to kick in. This should keep you going for a little while.'

He'd bought her a whole slew of magazines. One with puzzles in—he'd clearly remembered she liked the cross-words where you cracked the number code to work out the letters—and several glossies. Light, frivolous reading, the kind she hadn't indulged in for years because she'd been busy studying or working: the perfect thing for convalescence.

She heard what sounded like a knife on a chopping board—what *was* he doing?—and then he came back in, carrying another tray. This one contained a fresh jug of lemon barley water and a vase of flowers. Bright, cheerful orange gerberas.

He'd bought her flowers.

Just as he had when he'd been a student. They'd never been expensive or flashy, but he'd bought her flowers every Friday night without fail. Until the day Ethan had died, when he'd stopped doing anything at all.

Tears pricked her eyelids.

'Hey, they're meant to cheer you up. You're supposed to bring flowers to people who aren't well, to make them feel better,' he said, making light of it.

'Sorry.'

'No worries.' For a moment she thought he was going to reach out and touch her again. Hold her. And how she wanted him to.

But then he took a step back. 'If you want a shower, I've

put a fresh towel for you in the bathroom. My dressing-gown's behind the door. Help yourself to whatever you need.'

A shower.

Oh, Lord.

She was glad Kit's last comment had been made as he had been walking out of the room, because she was sure the memories must show on her face. Memories of sharing a shower with Kit. Squeezing into a tiny cubicle together, giggling because the fit was really too tight—and then not caring anyway, because once they'd started soaping each other it had quickly turned from laughter to passion.

They hadn't been able to keep their hands off each other.

Kit had lifted her against the tiles—and the momentary shock of cold tiles against her back had vanished with the heat his body had stoked in hers as he'd entered her.

Bad, bad, bad. She really had to get sex off the brain. Maybe a shower would wash a bit of common sense back into her head.

Kit heard the water running. Good. A shower would probably make Natalie feel better. The steam in the room would definitely help her to breathe more easily. He really ought to persuade her to sit with her face over a bowl of hot water and a towel over her head to keep the steam in and inhale the moist air for a few minutes.

He damped down the urge to join her in the shower. To stand under the running water and soap her all over, sluice the suds from her body, then make love with her until all their problems were forgotten.

It would be, oh, so easy.

Though they'd done that, and it hadn't worked. If

anything, it had made things even worse between them. He really needed to keep his hands to himself.

He shook himself and continued cooking dinner.

When he brought the tray of soup in to Natalie, she was propped up against the pillows, her hair still slightly damp from the shower. She smiled wanly at him. 'Hi.'

'Hi.' He sat down on the edge of the bed and settled the tray on her lap. 'I suppose this ought to be chicken soup, really, to help fight a virus. But I thought this might give you a lift—the colour as well as the taste—plus it's easy to swallow.'

Bright orange, it almost glowed against the plain white porcelain.

She took a sip, then frowned as she recognised the flavour. 'Carrot and orange?'

'Your mum's recipe, yeah. I've always liked it.' Tally herself had taught him to make it. Back in the days when they'd shared things like that—cooked each other meals, ate together, got distracted from doing the washing-up.

He stood up again, needing to put some space between them before he did something stupid. 'I'll be back in a bit.'

He returned a few minutes later with a plate of fluffy scrambled eggs, with roasted courgettes, mushrooms and peppers on the side. 'Thought I'd do you something soft, something that's easy on a sore throat.' She'd finished half the soup, he noted. Good. It was progress, of sorts.

'Where's yours?' she rasped.

'I'll eat later.' He didn't quite trust himself to eat with her. It'd bring back too many memories. And right now he needed to put her feelings first, not his.

When he came to collect her empty—well, half-empty—plate, her eyes were suspiciously red. 'What's wrong?' he asked. 'Didn't you like it?' Surely her tastes hadn't changed that much in the last six years?

'Not that. You're being so nice to me. I'm being wet. Sorry.'

A tear spilled over the edge of her lashes; he wiped it away with his thumb. 'You're not well, honey. Of course I'm going to be nice to you. What did you expect me to do, have a major fight with you?'

She dragged in a breath. 'Where are you sleeping tonight?'

Her voice was slightly quavery, he noticed. Was she worrying that he expected payment in kind for looking after her? 'On my sofa.'

'You're too tall. Be murder on your back.'

He shrugged. 'It's a sofa bed, Tally. Granted, it isn't as big as this is, and I wouldn't like to sleep on it permanently, but it won't do me any harm to sleep on it for a few nights. Until you're better.' He smiled. 'Don't worry, I'm not going to leap on you.' Even though there was nothing he'd like more than to have Natalie back in his bed. Back in his life. 'I just want you to get better. You need to rest. And this is the best place for you right now.'

She didn't answer, but scrubbed away another tear.

He sighed. 'Look, I may not be your husband any more and I know things went badly wrong between us—that I made a mess of things this time round, too—but I hope we can somehow find our way to being friends. Because I still care about you.' A lot. And he wanted to be a lot more than just her friend. But friendship would be a start. And a hell of a lot better than the cold war that had raged between them since the end of their marriage.

He took her tray away before he said something he knew he'd regret later. Now wasn't the time to pressure her.

But when she was better, maybe they'd be able to talk. Thrash things out. Come to some sort of compromise. Maybe—please, God—even agree to try again.

Natalie wrapped her arms round herself, willing the tears to stay back. Kit was looking after her—just like she'd needed him to be there when Ethan had died. Cherishing her. Putting her first. He was no longer the closed-up, shuttered-down man he'd become when they'd lost their baby. This was the Kit she'd fallen in love with. Strong and caring and dependable.

The Kit she'd never stopped loving.

And that was what scared her most. That she was falling for him all over again.

But she couldn't allow that to happen. Because this time, when it went wrong, there'd be nothing left.

CHAPTER TWELVE

KIT busied himself doing the washing-up. There had been a time when he and Natalie would have done this together. Like on lazy Sunday mornings when one of them had got up for long enough to stick some croissants in the oven to heat through and make a pot of coffee, then brought a tray back to bed. Where they'd skimmed through the Sunday papers, licked buttery crumbs off each other's fingers, and ended up making love.

Natalie would pull on one of his shirts—oh, how he'd loved seeing her in nothing but one of his shirts—and they'd pad barefoot to the kitchen, just long enough to wash up. Then they'd go back to bed again. They'd gloried in their time together, revelling in each other's bodies and the way they could make each other feel.

Even the memory made him hard. Made him want her, badly.

Sharing his space with Natalie again was strange. Familiar, yet at the same time not. They'd both changed over the last six years. Had different experiences, things they hadn't shared. There had been a time when they'd been so close they'd virtually read each other's minds. Now it was almost as if they'd met for the first time.

If Ethan hadn't died, things would have been so very different, Kit thought. They wouldn't be living separately in a tiny rented flat, neither of them putting down roots anywhere. They'd be living in a proper family house, maybe with two or three children, a house filled with warmth and love and laughter. After his shift at the hospital finished, he'd be coming *home*—not just to the place where he happened to live while he was in this post.

Right now Natalie was lying in his bed. Ill. Letting him look after her. So maybe her trust in him hadn't gone completely. Ah, how he ached to be there with her. Just lying beside her, being close to her, would be enough for him. But it wasn't fair to push it. Not while she was sick. He'd back off. Wait until she was better. And then maybe he could start to woo her properly.

He buried himself in paperwork for the rest of the evening, breaking off only to check if Natalie needed anything. The last time he checked, she was asleep. He stood in the doorway and watched her for a moment. Asleep, her face had lost the wariness he'd noticed when she was around him. And although she looked older now, he could still see the girl he'd fallen in love with twelve years ago.

The girl he still loved.

If only he could persuade her to give him another chance.

He padded into the room, took out clean clothes for himself in the morning, switched the bedside light off and closed the door behind him. Then he made up the sofa bed and sprawled out on it, though it was a long, long time before he could sleep.

The following morning, Kit woke with another headache. Lack of sleep, he guessed. Apart from the fact he'd had problems falling asleep the previous night, the sofa bed really wasn't that comfortable and he'd woken several times during the night. Though he'd make light of it if Tally asked. No way was he going to make her sleep on something so uncomfortable while she was ill. He showered quickly, dressed, then put out a fresh towel for Tally and restored order to his living room.

Assuming that he'd probably woken her, even though he'd tried to be quiet, he tapped lightly on the bedroom door.

''M awake,' she croaked.

He opened the door and peered round. 'Morning. How did you sleep?'

'Well. You?'

'Fine,' he fibbed. 'Want some breakfast?'

'Uh…' She grimaced.

She'd always been one for toast in the mornings. And toast would really hurt her right now. 'I could do you some porridge. Or fruit and yoghurt, if you'd rather have something cool.'

'Fruit would be good. Thanks,' she croaked.

'Go have a shower.' He rummaged in his wardrobe and found her another T-shirt. 'There are clean towels in the bathroom. I'll bring you a drink and some breakfast when you're ready.' Forestalling her protest, he added, 'I forgot to empty my washing machine yesterday. Your clothes are still soaking. So you'll have to stay put today as well.'

'Bossy,' she grumbled, but to his relief she did as he asked.

Her eyes widened when she saw her breakfast tray. 'Strawberries?'

So what if they were expensive, out of season? He knew she loved them. And raspberries. And blueberries. And orange juice that he'd squeezed into a glass only moments before. 'Vitamin C. Good for you.'

She wrinkled her nose. 'Flawed research. Doesn't really help colds.'

He grinned. He should've guessed that she'd say something like that. When they'd been students, she'd always read his journals and fenced with him on some subject or other. Helped him to see different sides of an argument, where to question and where to accept. 'You don't have a cold. You have a virus,' he retorted.

'Same difference.' But she smiled at him. A real smile, one that reached her eyes. Warm. The first time there'd been real warmth between them for years. 'Thank you, Kit.'

'My pleasure.' He smiled back. And left, before he could say something to stir up the antagonism between them and ruin it all.

Just before Kit left for his shift, he brought in a tray with a sandwich and a fresh jug of lemon barley. 'I'm on a late, so I bought you some pasta for dinner. Ravioli. All you have to do is take it out of the fridge, pierce the lid and nuke it in the microwave for a few minutes. Leave the washing-up. I'll do it later,' he said.

She was asleep when he came home—a little later than he'd intended, but there had been an emergency on the ward and he always preferred to stay around afterwards for an hour or so in case of a relapse. He really hadn't been avoiding her.

The kitchen was spotless. Tidy. Hmm. He'd left the breakfast things to air-dry. Everything had been put away neatly. Clearly she'd ignored his orders to do the washing-up—if she *had* eaten, that was. He checked the fridge, and the pasta had gone. Good. If she was eating, it meant she was definitely on the mend.

On the one hand, it pleased him.

On the other, it didn't. While Natalie was ill, she was staying with him—and he had the chance to get closer to her again. When she was better, he'd have to take her home, and they'd be back to living separate lives. It would be all too easy for the distance between them to grow again.

He showered and crawled into his uncomfortable bed. At least he was on an early tomorrow. Maybe they could talk the next evening.

The next morning followed the pattern of the previous one. Kit brought Natalie a hot drink and breakfast, made a fuss of her, brought in a lunch tray and disappeared on his shift.

And it really warmed her heart that he cared that much.

She was feeling better. Better enough to go home, really—although she was still coughing, her breathing had eased a bit. And she really didn't want to spend today in bed—it wasn't as if she was an invalid or seriously ill.

Kit had dried her clothes and left them in his bedroom for her. He'd ironed them, too, she noticed with a smile—and Kit loathed ironing. As a student, he'd always walked around in creased clothes, claiming there was no point in ironing things that would only get crumpled within a few minutes of wearing them. When they'd moved in together and he'd had to start wearing something respectable to work, Kit had agreed to wash their kitchen floor and clean the oven—her two most hated jobs—if she did the ironing.

They'd shared everything.

Until Ethan's death.

And then it had been as if they'd been stuck in different compartments. Aware of each other's existence but barely communicating.

Natalie showered, dressed and then pottered through into the living room. So this was where Kit was sleeping. Funny, although the room wasn't empty—there was a sofa bed, a television, a stereo and a desk housing a computer—the place didn't feel like Kit's home. It didn't feel lived in. There were no pot plants, no cushions, no little personal touches.

Except for the small framed photograph next to the anglepoise lamp on his desk. Her fingers shook as she picked it up and stared at it. Ethan. His first official photograph. Natalie remembered the photographer coming onto the ward every morning to take pictures of the newborns. She and Kit had already gone through two rolls of film by that point, but they'd had the photograph taken anyway. The one that came with a mount from the hospital. A big photograph for their wall, then smaller sizes to send to proud grandparents, aunts and uncles. Tiny ones that slipped perfectly inside a wallet or purse or credit-card holder. This was the photograph that she'd pasted inside Ethan's baby book—a book she'd kept meticulously during her pregnancy, with the scan pictures and measurements and all the family history. The book she'd planned to share with their son when he was older and curious about himself as a baby. Except she'd never had the chance.

She blinked away the tears. One thing that had never been in doubt was Kit's love for his son. He'd been so proud of their baby. The only time he'd left their bedside that first day had been to get the phone trolley so they could ring round the family with the news. And for long enough to order an enormous bouquet for her. It had arrived with a card handwritten by him that she'd never been able to throw away, even after the divorce. It was still in her keepsake box. Telling her how much he loved her, how proud he was of her.

She shook herself. That was the past. Over. She replaced the photograph on Kit's desk and spent the rest of the morning flicking channels on the television. Kit didn't even have a shelf of books in the house—strange, because he'd always been a great reader. There weren't many CDs either—though maybe he was using an MP3 player instead now. Something that would let him store a lot more music in a smaller format.

This place felt very temporary. Did that mean Kit was planning to move on soon? Was the job at St Joseph's just a stopgap while he waited for a paediatric consultant's post to come up somewhere?

Not that it was any of her business. Not any more. Not her place to ask either.

Natalie realised she'd fallen asleep in front of an old black-and-white film when she heard the front door open. There was a rap on the bedroom door, followed by a soft query. 'Natalie?'

'In here,' she mumbled, sitting up.

Kit walked into the living room, took one look at her and sighed. 'You were feeling better, you got up and now you feel atrocious. Right?'

'Mmm.' She hadn't expected to fall asleep. Or to feel this groggy and disoriented. It was only a virus, for goodness' sake. It shouldn't make her feel this awful.

He spread his hands. 'Now, as a doctor, you would tell your patient with a knockout virus to stay put until they feel better—and then spend one more day in bed to make absolutely sure they are over it. Especially because if they get up too early they risk a relapse. And then they should take it easy and not rush straight back to a demanding job. Right?'

'Yes,' she admitted.

'Good. Then I suggest you take your own advice. Go back to bed,' he said. 'I'll bring you a drink.'

'I'll make it,' she protested. 'You've been—'

'On duty,' he finished for her. 'I know. But the difference is, I don't have a virus. I'm perfectly fit and healthy. So it's not a problem.' To her shock, he actually ruffled her hair. It was the briefest of contacts, but it reminded her of the old days. Kit had always been physical with her. Connected.

'Go back to bed, honey,' he said softly. 'The more you rest now, the quicker you'll get better.'

And the quicker she'd be out of his hair?

No, that wasn't fair. He could have just left her at her own flat. In fact, he needn't even have taken her there himself. He could have put her in a taxi and just washed his hands of her. Instead, he'd brought her here, to his own flat. He'd looked after her, made sure she was eating properly. And she was being an ungrateful whiner. 'Thank you,' she muttered, feeling guilty and out of sorts at the same time.

She dragged herself back to bed. When Kit came in with a hot drink for her a few minutes later, she noticed that he looked strained.

'Are you OK?' she asked.

'Yeah, course.'

But his voice was clipped, tense. Something was definitely wrong. She hazarded a guess. 'Bad day at work?'

He shrugged. 'It was all right.'

Oh, no. She knew that tone. Remembered it well from the last few weeks of their marriage. Kit was upset about something, but he was keeping it locked away. Shutting her out. Again. Just when she'd been beginning to think that maybe he'd changed…

Well, she wasn't going to let him do this. Whatever it was, he needed to talk about it. Bring it out into the open and put it in perspective. She patted the empty space next to her on the bed. 'Sit. Tell me.'

For a moment he stared at her, and then he nodded. Kicked off his shoes. Sprawled next to her. 'OK, since you asked, I've had a hell of a day. If I tell you about it, it's going to upset you. And if I don't tell you about it, you're going to think I'm being like I was after Ethan died. Closed. And I'm not, Tally. I just don't want to…' He shook his head in frustration. 'I don't want to say something that's going to hurt you.'

Her first thought was that he'd met someone. That he didn't know how to tell her that he'd fallen in love and was going to get married again.

Then she shook herself. No, of course not. Apart from the fact that he wouldn't have brought her here if he was seeing someone else—Kit had never been the duplicitous sort—they were no longer married. It was none of her business if he'd found someone else.

Though she was pretty sure he'd been talking about work, not his personal life. His eyes were shadowed with pain.

And he'd said it would upset her.

Oh, God. Please, don't say it was little Kyra. Please, don't say she'd stopped responding to the cytotoxic drugs. 'Kyra?' she whispered. 'It's not Kyra? I didn't give her my virus? She's hasn't…' Oh, no. Please, no. She couldn't force the words out.

'No, so don't start worrying. She's doing OK, and she seems to be responding well to the treatment.' He gave her the briefest of smiles. 'And, thanks to you, she gets to go home for two whole hours on Christmas Day. I had a chat with Lenox about it and her Christmas wish will come true.'

'That's good.'

But something had happened, something to upset him. She wanted to make him feel better, soothe him the way he'd soothed her when she'd felt so rough earlier in the week. She stroked the hair back from his forehead. 'Tell me what's wrong,' she said softly. 'It's better out than in.'

'It's…' His mouth worked but no sound came out. Then he closed his eyes. Looked defeated, as if he didn't have the strength to deal with whatever it was any more. Well, that was OK. She was there.

'Tell me,' she said softly. 'Share. Lighten the load.'

He swallowed. 'We had a baby on the ward today. His mum brought him in with a virus. At first I thought it was another of our RSV cases. The baby had the usual symptoms for an upper respiratory tract infection—poor breathing, a bit of cynosis round the mouth. But I had a bad feeling about it.'

A doctor's gut reaction. Yeah. She was beginning to develop that, too.

'The heart rate was way too fast. I listened, and there was an S4 gallop.'

She knew what that pointed to. 'Myocarditis?' she asked, her voice low.

'Yeah.'

She took his hand and squeezed it. 'Is this your first case since Ethan?'

He shook his head. 'Far from it. But it gets to me every time. I think I'm being professional about it, and I'm absolutely fine on the ward. Nobody would ever guess what it means to me. But as soon as I'm off duty…it all comes back. Every single second. Ethan's face, the way his breathing got worse and worse, the moment he fell asleep

for ever. The moment the sun burned out.' His expression
was bleak as he opened his eyes and looked at her. 'When's
it ever going to stop hurting, Tally?'

'I don't know.' Instinctively, she slid her arms round
him. Pillowed his head on her breasts. Stroked his hair and
just held him close. His arms wrapped round her, but this
time there wasn't the usual sexual frisson between them.
This time, she was holding him. Comforting him. And for
once he was actually leaning on her. Letting her in. Sharing
his pain. Accepting that you didn't have to be strong and
in control of your feelings all the time.

It wasn't for long—'I'll go fix dinner,' he muttered,
clearly thinking he'd been weak in her eyes, and was embarrassed about it—but it was a start.

Maybe there was hope for them yet.

CHAPTER THIRTEEN

THE following evening, Kit came home in a much better mood.

'Had a good day?' Natalie asked.

He smiled. 'Yeah. We had one of the best cases ever on the ward today.'

She patted the bed. 'Sit down and tell me about it.'

He looked at her for a moment, as if about to refuse, then kicked off his shoes and sat down next to her, leaning back against the pillows.

Just as he'd done in the days when he'd been a house officer and she'd been heavily pregnant, too tired to wait up properly for him but not wanting to go to sleep until he'd got home from his shift.

'We had this little boy in. Billy. Three years old and a right little scamp. Anyway, he's been limping for the last three months.'

Natalie frowned. Why was Kit smiling? How could this be a good case if a child was ill? Hurt?

'Lenox knew he was coming in today and asked me to see him for a second opinion because the case had him puzzled—actually, young Billy would've been a good case for you.' There was a glint of mischief in Kit's eyes. 'Quick *viva* for you. What causes limping?'

'A stone or something sharp in the shoe, badly fitting shoes or maybe a foreign body in the foot.'

'Nope. Remember, this child has been limping for three months—and his mum brought him within a couple of days of the limp starting.'

It went without saying that Billy's mum had checked his shoes for a stone. And if the cause had been a foreign body—a thorn, or even the after-effects, like poor Harry a few weeks ago—it would have been picked up as soon as he'd come in for examination. And ill-fitting shoes could be crossed out for the same reasons. So that ruled out the three most obvious causes.

Something developmental maybe? 'He's been limping for just three months? His mum didn't notice anything before, not even the slightest hint of problems with walking?'

'Nope. Not a thing. And she's very observant,' Kit added.

Natalie thought aloud. 'It's unlikely to be hip displacement, then.' She frowned. 'Is Billy in any pain at all? Has he complained of any aches, anything hurting, a pushing or a squeezing pain?'

'Apparently not.'

'Is he accident prone?' she asked.

'A bit.' Kit looked interested. 'Why?'

'It might be an undiagnosed greenstick fracture that had mended badly.'

Kit nodded. 'Good call—and I'm impressed that you're thinking outside the box, not just limiting yourself to the obvious. That gets you an extra mark, Dr Wilkins. But the X-rays show absolutely nothing wrong.'

'How about mild cerebral palsy, but nobody had picked up on it yet simply because it was so mild?' she suggested.

'He wasn't a late walker, there are no signs of CNS lesions and there are no other symptoms.' Kit laughed. 'There's definitely nothing wrong with his speech, I can tell you that—he chatted nineteen to the dozen to me. Oh, and he was a full-term baby.'

Which ruled out most of the possible indicators of cerebral palsy. Natalie folded her arms and drummed her fingers on her elbow. 'Unlikely to be CP, then. How about Duchenne muscular dystrophy?'

'Good try, but nope.' Kit shook his head. 'OK, I'll tell you a little bit more. Billy's had every test you can imagine. Bloods—that's hormone assays as well as full blood count, U and Es and what have you—X-rays, ultrasound... And they've all been negative.'

Natalie was beginning to see why Lenox had been puzzled. There was no obvious cause for a limp. And if their extremely experienced consultant couldn't work out what the problem was, how on earth did Kit think that a house officer who was still wet behind the ears would come up with a diagnosis? If it wasn't physical, then maybe... 'Is it psychosomatic perhaps?' she asked. 'Maybe something had happened at home to upset him? Maybe it's a form of attention-seeking?'

'No. We're talking about well-adjusted little boy who lives in big, noisy, happy family—a family who loves him to bits, I might add.'

The kind Natalie had grown up in. The kind she'd wanted for her own children. 'Uh-huh.'

'I thought maybe his tendons had retracted in the back of his leg, and that was what caused the limp. How would you deal with that?'

'Refer him to a surgeon to have them released,' Natalie suggested.

'Or botox injections to relax them,' Kit said. He grinned. 'You know, I never thought just the threat of a needle could cure a limp so fast.'

She frowned. 'I'm not with you.'

'I'd explained it to his parents while he was playing— what I thought the problem might be and how we could manage it. But I always like to talk to my patients, too— they may be small but they still have a right to know what's happening to them. So then I sat down next to the toy box and explained to Billy that we were going to have to give him an operation or maybe a very special type of injection to help stop him limping. And then he piped up, "Will an injection cure Grandpa Henry, too?"'

'Who's Grandpa Henry?' Natalie asked.

'His mum's dad. Who just so happens to have a limp— he has arthritis.' Kit laughed. 'Apparently, young Billy had just been copying his grandfather.'

'No.' Natalie stared at him in disbelief and amusement. 'You're kidding.'

'I'm serious. There was absolutely nothing wrong with him. He was just copying his grandfather and seeing how it felt to have a limp.'

'For three *months*?'

'Yep. I couldn't quite believe it either. He kept it up for three whole months.'

'The little…' Natalie laughed, shaking her head. 'What did his mum say?'

'She wasn't sure whether to be relieved that he wasn't going to have to go through an operation or whether to throttle him for worrying her sick!' Kit's lips quirked. 'Poor woman. She was so embarrassed. Lucky for her, I have a sense of humour. So does Lenox. And I'd never yell at a parent for wasting our time anyway. Often the parents are the first ones to pick up that there's a problem. And I'd much, much rather it was a false alarm than for things to progress beyond the point where we can treat them.' He smiled again. 'My money's on young Billy becoming a famous actor in about twenty years' time. He could be the new Brando—a method actor who really becomes the character. You know: gains weight if he has to for the role.' He chuckled. 'Or, in this case, walks with a limp for three months.'

Natalie smiled back. 'Certainly sounds like it.'

'It's not all tragedy in paediatrics. Yes, we get sad cases— there will always be some we can't help.' He was clearly thinking of their son, because his face clouded for a moment. 'But there are many, many more we can help get better. And then there are the ones that go down in legend. The ones where you only have to mention the patient's name and the staff have to try really hard to keep a straight face.'

She loved this side of Kit—when he really opened up to her and told her what he enjoyed about his job. Like the days when he'd first qualified. He'd never broken patient confidentiality, but he'd come home and chatted to her about his day. Just as she'd told him about hers. And she wanted to keep him talking now. 'What sort of cases?'

'I think my favourite one was when I was doing a stint in the emergency department as their paediatric specialist. This little boy came in—apparently, he was a bit accident-prone anyway, and his file was enormous. He'd been in with a foreign body up his nose, in his ears—even swallowed at one point. He found his dad's superglue and managed to glue his fingers together. He'd fallen over so many times that his mum was terrified she'd be on an abuse register. You name it, he'd done it. But that particular day he showed up with a potty stuck on his head.'

'A potty?'

Kit grinned. 'I know, I know—the classic case is a saucepan stuck on a kid's head. But his mum had already sussed that one out and kept a child lock on her saucepan cupboard to make sure he didn't try being a robot or something and get his head stuck in a saucepan.'

'But how on earth did he get his head stuck in a potty?' Natalie asked.

Kit chuckled. 'Apparently, he tripped over the cat and landed headfirst in his brother's potty.'

'Ow. Please tell me it was an empty potty,' Natalie said faintly.

Kit's grin broadened. 'Nope. Think worst-case scenario. His mum was just cleaning up his little brother before she emptied the potty. They were in the bathroom when she heard this wail, and rushed out to see her eldest with some rather unusual headgear.'

'Oh, no! That's awful.' Natalie was torn between sympathy and laughter.

'Let's just say her face was a bit red when she explained. Poor woman. She probably sees the funny side of it now, but at the time she was frantic—obviously she needed to get the potty off her son's head and get him cleaned up, too, but it was stuck. He wasn't too happy either—he was yelling and creating the whole time, and we just couldn't get him to calm down.'

'Well, it can't have been too pleasant for him. And I can't even begin to imagine the smell. How did you get it off?' Natalie asked.

'We had to put a warm damp cloth over the top of the potty. It was plastic, so obviously the material would expand with heat and we'd be able to get it off, but we had to be careful with the temperature—if the cloth was too hot it'd make the plastic melt and make the situation even worse. We replaced the warm cloth every ten minutes or so and smeared cold baby oil right up under the rim, as far as we could reach. Eventually, the contrast between the warmth of the cloth and the coldness of the oil did the trick—the potty expanded and we managed to get it off.' He grimaced. 'It took an hour, and the poor little scrap was left with oil and poo all over his hair. We cleaned him up before we sent him home. But that's one episode I bet he never lives down!'

'It's something his mum can remind him about whenever he's being a really stroppy teenager and she wants to take him down a peg or two,' Natalie said.

'Definitely.' He smiled at her. 'So are you enjoying paediatrics?'

'Yes. I'm doing an emergency department rotation next, but I want to come back to paediatrics.'

'It's really rewarding,' Kit agreed.

'Do you ever miss not going into surgery?' The question was out before she could stop it.

He shrugged. 'Not really. I mean, yes, there's a real adrenaline rush in surgery. You're working against the clock, and you're taking risks—calculated risks, but there's still a possibility your patient won't make it out of Theatre. Everything depends on your skill, and that of your team. But there isn't the same…I dunno.' He wrinkled his nose. 'I think it's the contact, really. I like seeing my patients. I like it when they come back for a review and I can sign them off, and I can see how much they've changed since the last review. I like getting to know them, seeing the tots turn into bouncy little people with minds of their own. Or the shy young children blossoming in their teenage years. No, I don't regret the change at all.' He tipped his head on one side. 'How about you? Do you regret giving up teaching?'

'Yes and no. I liked working with the kids, teaching them to really think about what they were looking at and how to structure a proper argument. But I'm glad I do this now.' Natalie admitted. 'There's something special about being able to help people, make things right again.'

'Yes,' Kit said softly. 'There is.' And then he climbed off the bed. 'I'd better go and sort dinner. See you in a bit.'

Natalie would quite happily have foregone food for more time with him. Time they'd spent laughing—the first time in years they'd laughed together. Talked about what they were doing and how they really felt.

But maybe she was just hoping for too much.

The following day, Natalie was feeling much brighter. She was up, showered and dressed before Kit got up, and had the coffee on and the table set ready for breakfast before she even heard him go into the bathroom.

Kit blinked in surprise as he walked into the kitchen, his hair still wet from the shower. 'Wow. What's this?'

'You made a fuss of me while I was ill. This is the least I could do,' Natalie said, pouring him a coffee and switching the toaster on.

'Thanks.' He sat down and took a sip. 'You sound a lot better. Your voice is almost back. And you've got some colour in your cheeks again.'

'I *am* better. I'm going back to work today,' she said.

He shook his head. 'Don't rush it. You've got two days off anyway.'

She raised an eyebrow. 'How do you know?'

'Checked the roster.' He lifted a shoulder casually. 'You must be dying to have your own space back again.'

Ouch. Whatever she said could be taken the wrong way. If she said yes, he'd think she was desperate to put space between them. If she said no, she'd be throwing herself at him. He'd slept on his sofa-bed every single night since she'd stayed here—even the night after he'd talked to her about the baby with myocardia. The night she'd half expected him to come to her bed, seek comfort in her arms.

He hadn't.

Which meant he really did see her just as a platonic friend now. Not his life partner.

'It'd be nice to have my wardrobe back,' she said, trying for lightness.

'I would've gone to your place and brought you some things back, if you'd said.'

'I know. But you've already done enough for me. Thanks, Kit. I appreciate it.'

He didn't meet her eyes. 'That's what friends are for, isn't it?'

Yes. But they'd once been more than friends. A lot more.

'I'm on a late today. I'll drive you back to your place when you're ready.'

It sounded as if he wanted his space back, too. 'OK. I'll just strip the bed—'

He lifted one hand to stop her. 'Leave it, Natalie. I'll sort it out later.'

She didn't bother with the rest of her breakfast, and it

didn't take her long to pack. 'Maybe you should drop me at the hospital. I can pick up my car,' Natalie said.

'No need. I moved your car the other day.'

How?

As if she'd spoken the question aloud, he said, 'I drove it to your place, then caught a taxi back to the hospital.'

She flushed. 'Thank you. Um, I'll reimburse you for the taxi.'

'No need.'

She hated this sudden awkwardness between them. But right now she couldn't think of any way to change it.

He drove her back to her flat. Saw her to the door. 'Take care of yourself,' he said with a smile. A smile that was just that little bit too bright. And which meant he was shutting her out again.

'Thanks for everything.'

'No worries. See you at work.'

And that was it. He was gone.

Well, what had she expected? That he'd stay for coffee? She knew he was on duty shortly. And, knowing Kit, he wanted to drop in to the intensive care unit and see how the baby with myocarditis was doing.

Natalie let herself into her flat. Weird. This place didn't feel like a home either—even though, unlike Kit's flat, hers was full of family photographs and pot plants and books and flowers. It just felt…empty, without him. Which was stupid. He'd never lived here. He hadn't even spent a whole night here—they'd had sex and she'd thrown him out.

There was a heap of mail on the doormat. Christmas cards, she thought, her heart aching as she scooped them up. No doubt full of round-robin letters from friends she only heard from at this time of year. Letters full of 'proud mummy' moments—moments she'd once dreamed of writing about in her annual catch-ups.

Christmas just *sucked*. And if she put the radio on it'd be some Christmas song or other, either a bouncy one saying how wonderful life was or a sad one wishing their loved ones would be home for Christmas.

Her baby hadn't made it home for Christmas.

She sighed, put her mail on the table and made herself a strong cup of coffee. This was crazy. She had a job she loved, family she loved, friends. She ought to be delighted with the way her life was right now. Why on earth did she feel so lonely, so empty?

Though she knew the answer. It was because Kit wasn't there. He'd dropped her off only a few minutes ago and already she missed him.

Maybe she should call him. Tell him how she felt. Ask him to give their relationship another try.

But he'd already suggested that and she'd knocked him back. And although he'd looked after her when she'd been ill, he'd made it very clear it was on a friends-only basis.

So just where did they go from here?

Right now she didn't have any answers. Just a cup of coffee and an ache in her heart and a wish that things were different.

CHAPTER FOURTEEN

IT FELT odd to Kit that evening, coming home to find his flat dark and empty. Although Tally had only stayed for a few days, he'd grown used to having her there. He'd enjoyed coming home to her.

Though he'd noted that as soon as she had felt better, she hadn't been able to get away fast enough.

Kit sighed inwardly. He wouldn't see Natalie again until after Christmas now. She was off duty tomorrow, and he was off duty for the two days after that—days when he'd go south to pay a fleeting visit to his parents to drop off the family's Christmas presents and pretend to his brothers that of course everything in his busy-busy-busy life was fine—and then it would be Christmas. Tally was bound to spend the holidays at her parents' home. She'd always been very family oriented.

And then it would be the new year.

Time for a new start.

Kit was beginning to think his would have to be in another hemisphere, let alone another hospital.

'Kit!' Nicole Rodgers smiled at her son as she opened the front door. 'I wasn't sure if you were coming.'

'I promised I would.' Even though he really hadn't felt

like it. 'I wouldn't let you down. And I'd be the meanest uncle in the world if I didn't bring the kids their presents in time for Christmas morning—especially as it's too late for the last post before Christmas.'

She squeezed his arm briefly. 'I know it's a tough time of year for you. Too many memories.'

'I'm fine,' Kit protested.

'You don't look it.' She ushered him into the kitchen and switched the kettle on. 'You look as if you haven't slept properly for weeks.'

Kit didn't answer. How come his mother was suddenly so perceptive?

'So how's the new job?' she asked.

'Fine.'

'Right, and that's why you sound so underwhelmed. What's the problem? A consultant who wants to keep all the responsibility and can't delegate?'

'No, Lenox is great. I love working on the ward. It's a good team.'

His mother busied herself making tea. 'So it's a nurse who won't take no for an answer, then?'

When he didn't reply, she sighed. 'Kit, I know you were badly hurt by what happened with Natalie. But you can't live in the shadows for the rest of your life, thinking of all the might-have-beens. You have to make a new life. Move on.'

Move on. What Natalie herself had suggested. Kit sighed. 'That's easier said than done.'

'You need to get out and meet people,' Nicole said authoritatively. 'You can't just work, work, work all the time. What you need is to find someone to share your life with. Join a club.' She put a mug of coffee in front of him. 'Or a dating agency—one of those places that caters to people who are too busy to find themselves a partner. They'll match you up with someone who has interests in common with you. There's no stigma in that sort of thing nowadays.'

Kit stared into his coffee. 'That isn't what I meant.'

'Then what do you mean, darling?' she asked.

He might as well tell her straight. 'I'm working with Natalie now.'

Nicole frowned. 'What, she's one of these teachers who work on the paediatric ward with children who are in long term? I thought she was a history teacher?'

'Not any more. She's a house officer on my ward.'

'Good Lord.' Nicole pulled out a chair from the scrubbed pine table. 'I mean, I always knew she was clever—but how?'

'Same way as I did, I guess,' Kit said dryly. 'Five years at university, and then a year in pre-reg.'

Nicole gave him a look that said very clearly, Don't give me that smart-alec response. 'And she's specialising in paediatrics?'

'Mmm-hmm.' Kit pre-empted his mother's next question. 'For the same reason I switched specialties, I guess.'

Nicole paused before asking delicately, 'And how are you both coping with this? Working together?'

'OK.'

To Kit's surprise, she reached out and squeezed his hand. 'You never really got over her, did you? If you ask me, I'd say you're still in love with her.' At his half-shrug, she asked, 'Does she know?'

'No.'

'Do you know how she feels?'

'No.' Which was the problem. Sometimes he thought it was going to work out, that they'd have another chance—

and then they were back on opposite sides of the fence. He wasn't sure whether he was just trying to see something that wasn't there, or whether Natalie was running scared, or what.

All he knew was that he was miserable. Bone-deep miserable. And he missed her.

'You need to talk to her,' Nicole said gently. 'The way you should have done years ago.'

Kit frowned. 'Let me get this straight. You're telling me to talk to her, not to run like hell in the opposite direction?' He shook his head. 'Tally always thought you disapproved of her. That she wasn't academic enough for you.'

Nicole looked surprised. 'No, not at all. I just thought you were both too young to get married. You were both still students, remember. I thought you both needed to grow up a little, see more of the world before you settled down.'

'And Ethan?'

Nicole sighed and took a swig of her coffee. 'I admit, when you told me you were expecting, I thought it was bad timing, even though I know he wasn't planned. You were only just in your houseman year and up to your eyes in your job— you really weren't ready for the responsibility of a family.'

'So you disapproved.' Kit stared at the table. It looked as if Natalie was right about that, then.

Nicole shook her head. 'Ethan was my first grandchild. Who couldn't love their grandchild to bits? And he looked so very much like you as a baby.'

The last words sounded choked. Kit glanced at his mother, and was shocked to see her eyes filling with tears. As an oncology specialist, Nicole Rodgers was completely unflappable and cool at work. Kit had always thought her a bit that way at home, too, since he'd met Tally's family. Nicole had never been as warm and demonstrative as

Tally's mother. Though Kit had sometimes wondered if it was to do with the fact that she had four sons, whereas Tally's mother had three daughters.

He reached over and squeezed her hand. 'Mum, I…' Ah, hell. Now he was choking up, too.

She blinked the tears away. 'I know. My loss was nothing compared to yours. But I was sorry when you and Natalie split up. I wish now I'd gone to see her. Talked to her. Made her realise that although I was only an in-law, I was still there for her if she needed me.'

'But you didn't stay in touch with her,' Kit said. Not the way he'd stayed in touch with Tally's parents.

Nicole shook her head. 'I didn't think she wanted me to. And I wasn't going to push in where I wasn't needed.'

'So if,' Kit asked carefully, 'I could persuade her to give me a second chance…'

'I'd welcome her back with open arms,' Nicole said, 'if she could make you happy again.'

Kit smiled. 'Let's just say I'm working on it.' His smile faded. 'And if it doesn't work out, I might need to work abroad for a bit.'

'I hope,' Nicole said, 'for all our sakes, that doesn't happen.'

On Christmas Day, Tally woke at stupid o'clock to find a familiar dragging feeling in her abdomen. Her period had arrived. Like clockwork. She'd got her Christmas wish, then. She wasn't pregnant.

So why the hell did she feel so miserable about it?

As for her other wish…well, that was just a pipe dream. It wasn't going to happen.

She went into work early—she thought she may as well,

seeing as she was awake and didn't have anything better to do with her time. She helped the nurses to sort out the Christmas parcels for the children on the ward; money collected by the Friends of the Hospital had paid for all the patients to have a small gift. Debbie told her, just before the ward round on Christmas morning, that the most senior male doctor on the ward donned the Santa suit and walked round the bays, saying 'Ho, ho, ho' in a deep, jolly voice and giving each child a parcel. And all the nursing staff got a Christmas kiss under the mistletoe.

'Sounds like fun,' Natalie said, forcing her voice to sound bright and cheerful.

'It makes the day at bit easier for the parents,' Debbie said. 'It isn't much of a Christmas, torn between a family at home and a child in here. Wanting to be with both, and wearing themselves out in the process.'

'Mmm,' Natalie said, not trusting herself to say any more, and busied herself with preparation for the ward round.

Kit glanced at the roster board and did a double-take. He'd had no idea that Natalie would be working here on Christmas Day. He hadn't even looked at the roster sheets, because he'd assumed that she would spend the day in the Cotswolds with her parents and her sisters.

Ah, well. They'd just have to be civil to each other. It was Christmas after all. Though he had no intention of kissing her under the mistletoe. One touch of her mouth against his and he knew his self-control would be in shreds. They'd already made enough of a stir at the Hallowe'en do—the last thing he wanted was to give the hospital grapevine another juicy morsel.

The Santa suit was in Lenox's office. Kit climbed into it, added the beard and went in search of the presents.

* * *

'Ho, ho, ho. Merry Christmas, children.'

Natalie blinked hard. That most definitely wasn't Lenox's voice. And she hadn't been expecting to hear Kit: she'd assumed that he would be going south for Christmas. Spending the holidays with his family.

She still hadn't quite taken it in by the time he walked over to Debbie and held the mistletoe over her. 'Merry Christmas, Sister,' he said, giving her a resounding peck on the cheek.

Debbie laughed, and gave him an equally smacking kiss in return. 'Merry Christmas, Santa.'

Kit repeated the act with every nurse on the ward. And the auxiliary staff. And the mums.

Which left just Natalie.

He came to a stop in front of her, his blue eyes glittering. 'Merry Christmas, Dr Wilkins,' he said softly.

'Merry Christmas, Santa.' Her voice was actually shaking.

The briefest, briefest touch of his lips against her cheek, and he was gone.

Even so, it left her knees weak.

Avoiding the curious looks of the nurses, Natalie escaped to the staff kitchen for a much-needed cup of coffee.

'I thought I might find you here.' Kit walked into the kitchen a few minutes later and made himself a cup of coffee.

'I didn't realise you were on duty today,' she said.

'Snap.' He pulled back the hood of the Santa outfit and removed the beard. 'I thought you'd be at home with your family.'

She shook her head. 'Christmas is a time for kids. We've got staff who have children—I'd rather give them the chance of spending the day with their families instead of coming here and missing out.'

Meaning that she didn't have anything to miss out on? Yeah, he could identify with that.

Kit stared at her. She looked as miserable as he felt. Maybe…?

Well, he had nothing left to lose. He'd ask her. It might mean that his notice period over the next few weeks would be awkward in the extreme—but, then again, it was Christmas. A time he'd once thought held magic. If he didn't ask, he'd never know. And if he held back now, he might just be missing out on the rest of his life.

'I overheard you talking to Kyra about your Christmas wish.'

Her eyes widened. 'That was none of your business.'

He ignored the comment. 'Are you going to tell me what it was?'

'That everyone on the ward has a very happy Christmas.'

Which was what she'd told Kyra. He didn't buy it. At all. 'I meant the real one,' he said softly.

'No point. Because it's not going to happen.' She leaned back against her chair. 'I'm glad I saw you, actually. You asked me to let you know if… Well. The answer's no. I'm not pregnant.'

She was striving for coolness. He could see that. But her lower lip wobbled. Not for long—but long enough to give him hope. Was she disappointed that they hadn't made a baby? That they hadn't had a second chance?

He pulled up a chair next to hers. 'Want to know my Christmas wish, Tally?'

She wouldn't meet his eyes. 'No.'

'I'm going to tell you anyway. I should have told you this a long, long time ago.' He reached out, took her hand and held it between his. 'I wish I could have saved our son.

I wish I could have saved our marriage. I wish we had more children now—that we were a proper family. The way we wanted it to be, back when we were eighteen and we realised that we'd found the one we wanted to be with for the rest of our lives.'

Natalie was trembling, but he wasn't going to let her go. Not yet.

'But you can't change the past,' he said softly. 'I couldn't save Ethan. Our marriage blew apart. And now we're both on our own. Lonely.'

A muscle flickered in her jaw, as if she was trying not to cry. It looked as if he'd hit the nail on the head.

Please, God, let this work.

'So I have another wish.' He swallowed hard. 'What I wish, more than anything else in the world, is that we could have a second chance. That we could try again and make a real go of our relationship. Make it the marriage it was supposed to be.'

Slowly, slowly, she met his gaze. 'You want us to…?'

'Get back together. Get married again.' He took a deep breath. 'Yes. I never stopped loving you, Natalie. Even though I tried to block it out with work. I tried dating— but it never worked because they just weren't you. You're the love of my life and nobody will ever match up to you. Ever. And last week, when you stayed with me…it was the first time in years that I felt as if I were coming home. Because I was coming home to you, not just to an empty space filled with memories and regrets.' He took a chance. 'And I think it was the same for you. Wasn't it?'

Her breath hitched. 'You shut me out. You wouldn't talk to me. I needed you and you just weren't there.'

'I know. It's something I'm not proud of. Something I

regret from the bottom of my heart. I'm sorry. And all I can do is ask you to forgive me—because it won't happen again.'

She looked torn. Tempted and scared at the same time. 'How can you be so sure?'

'Because I'm a different person now, Tally. I'm older. Wiser, I hope. I deal with things in a different way now. You might have to prod me occasionally—I'm not perfect and I'm never going to be—but swear I'll try never to shut you out again. And if you just talk to me, we can make it work.'

'What if…?' Her breath hitched.

'If we're not blessed with another baby?' He drew her hand to his mouth and kissed each finger in turn. 'That's OK. Because we'll still have each other. And if we *are* lucky enough to have another child, he or she won't take Ethan's place.' He could guess her other fears. They'd be similar to his own. 'It's very, very unlikely our baby will have the same problems as Ethan. But if something bad does happen— well, we'll get through it together. I won't run away into my work. I'll face it with you. Hand in hand. And we'll get through whatever bad stuff life throws at us—just as we'll celebrate the good stuff, too. Together.' His hand tightened round hers again. 'Take a chance on me, Tally. Take a chance on *us*.'

'Put all the bad memories behind us and start again.'

'Yeah. It's going to take time, I know that. And we'll have bad days as well as good, days when we'll fight. But we'll get through them because we'll be together.' His eyes held hers. 'I love you, Tally. I never stopped.'

'Neither did I.' A tear trickled down her cheek. 'Do you really want to know what my Christmas wish was?'

'What?'

'The same as yours.'

He lifted one hand to wipe the tear from her cheek. 'Then let's make it come true. For each other.'

She shook her head. 'Your family won't approve.'

'I think,' Kit said, 'you might be surprised. I talked about you to my mother when I went back to Surrey on my off-duty.'

Natalie looked worried. 'And?'

'Same problem as me. You didn't talk it through together. Do you know, she still carries a picture of Ethan in her purse?' His fingers tightened on hers. 'She thought we were too young to get married and needed to grow up a bit, but she liked you. She's just...not very good at showing it. I dunno. Maybe it's because she had four sons and no daughters. She didn't know how to respond to you.'

'Maybe,' Natalie said softly.

'And she regrets not coming to see you after Ethan died and telling you that even though she was just an in-law, she was there if you needed her. She didn't want to push in because she thought you didn't want her.'

Natalie looked stunned. 'I had no idea.'

'Neither did I. I think maybe my family needs to learn a bit about talking. And sharing.' He smiled at her. 'You were a teacher. A good one. Would you consider taking on a new pupil?'

She opened her arms to him. 'Yes.'

Neither of them heard the kitchen door open. Or the wolf whistles. Or noticed Debbie shooing the nursing staff out again. All they could focus on was each other. And the feeling of coming home. For good.

EPILOGUE

Eighteen months later

KIT sat on the side of Natalie's bed, cradling their newborn daughter. 'She looks just like you,' he said with a smile.

'She definitely has your chin, though.' Natalie stroked the baby's soft dark hair. 'Carolyn Nicole Rodgers.' They'd decided to name their daughter after both their mothers. 'Our little girl.'

Kit looked at his wife, picking up the sadness in her voice. 'Hey. She's not a replacement for Ethan. Nobody will ever take his place, even if we have sons in the future. He'll always be our firstborn, and we'll tell Carolyn all about her big brother.'

Natalie's eyes were dark with worry. 'Kit, you don't think…?' She broke off, shaking her head, as if trying to dismiss it.

He guessed what she was worrying about immediately—the question that had flashed into his own mind, too—and set about reassuring her. 'Firstly, Carolyn's a summer-born baby. She's unlikely to come into contact with the same viruses in the summer that you get in the winter. Secondly, even if she does pick up Coxsackie from somewhere, it won't necessarily lead to cardiomyopathy in her case. It doesn't always cause it. Ethan might have had a heart problem anyway, and we just hadn't had a chance to pick that up. Carolyn is going to be absolutely fine. I checked her over myself.' His mouth twitched. 'Of course, if you want a *second* consultant's opinion, we could wait for Lenox to do his round.'

Nicole smiled. 'He's been a consultant for a lot longer than you have.'

'Cheek! I'll have you know I'm perfectly competent.' Kit leaned over to kiss his wife. 'She's doing well, Natalie. Everything's going to be fine. Because our Christmas wish has come true.'

'We've been lucky,' she said softly.

'And we're only going to get luckier. Because we're together.'

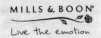

MILLS & BOON®

Live the emotion

Medical romance™

THE SURGEON'S MEANT-TO-BE BRIDE
by Amy Andrews

Nurse Harriet Remy and her surgeon husband
Guillaume thought they had the perfect marriage.
Then Harriet's fertility came under threat and her
subsequent desire for a baby came between them.
After a year apart, Gill still adores his wife, and on a
final overseas aid mission with her, decides this will
also become a mission to save their marriage – and
keep his wife by his side…for ever.

A FATHER BY CHRISTMAS *by Meredith Webber*

Neonatologist Sophie Fisher is bowled over by her
new boss's strength and kindness. She hasn't yet
told Gib that Thomas, the little boy in her care, is
actually her nephew, and that she is trying to find
his father. Gib is dedicated to his patients and not
looking for love – though there is something about
Sophie that is changing his mind. Then he makes a
discovery about Thomas…

A MOTHER FOR HIS BABY *by Leah Martyn*

Dr Brady McNeal is hoping a new life for him and his
tiny son will be just what they need, and the Mount
Pryde Country Practice seems like a small slice of
heaven – especially when he finds that he is working
with GP Jo Rutherford. The attraction between
Brady and Jo is undeniable. Soon Brady is wishing
that Jo had a more permanent role in his life…

On sale 1st December 2006